TABOR EVANS

LONGARM

AND THE NEVADA NYMPHS

JOVE BOOKS, NEW YORK

LONGARM AND THE NEVADA NYMPHS

A Jove Book / published by arrangement with
the author

PRINTING HISTORY
Jove edition / December 1998

The Penguin Putnam Inc. World Wide Web site address is
http://www.penguinputnam.com

ISBN: 0-515-12411-7

A JOVE BOOK®
Jove Books are published by The Berkley Publishing Group,
a member of Penguin Putnam Inc.,
375 Hudson Street, New York, New York 10014.
JOVE and the "J" design are trademarks
belonging to Jove Publications, Inc.

PRINTED IN THE UNITED STATES OF AMERICA

10 9 8 7 6 5 4 3 2 1

Chapter 1

Longarm peeked out the door of the empty storefront, and looked toward the big stone house that stood at the end of the dusty street like some sort of monument to the dead ghost town. There was nothing to be seen except a couple of rifles protruding from second-story windows. Other than that, there was no activity anywhere.

Longarm knew the stone house well. He had reconnoitered it from every direction, and it was as solid as a fortress. He didn't reckon there was any way that one man was going to get past the rifle fire, somehow breach the stone walls of the house, and get at the Hunsacker clan that was holed up inside. He understood that they had plenty of food, plenty of ammunition, and plenty of time. He was at his own discretion to either wait them out, go for help, or just go.

He moved across the street and closer to the house, hurrying through the dust and tumbleweeds of the main street, stepping up on the rotting boardwalk and ducking into what had formerly been the sheriff's office. The town, at one time, had been named Lodestar, after the main silver mine that had given it life. But when the silver had run out, so had the miners and so had the storekeepers and so had everyone else. Now, it was just so many framed buildings rotting in the dry, high air of Nevada.

All except for the stone house, which had belonged to the mine's owner. The man had gotten out with a considerable fortune, enough that he could walk away from such a sight as the eight- or-nine-room house he'd built to celebrate his success.

Longarm hunkered down by a window in the sheriff's office, where he could see the best part of the stone mansion, as he got out a cigarillo and lit it, wishing he had a drink. His whiskey was back in his saddlebags at the livery at the opposite end of the street from the stone house. He reckoned he could do without it. He had a gallon canteen of water with him, and he eased it off his shoulder and took a long drink. He was armed with his .44-caliber revolver in his cross-draw holster. Besides that, he had his carbine, which also fired .44-caliber to eliminate the need for different types of ammunition. He also had a .44-caliber double-barreled derringer attached to one end of his watch chain. It had saved his life more than once.

Longarm wanted to cuss his boss, United States Marshal Billy Vail, for the trouble that he now found himself in, but he had to admit that it was nobody's fault but his own. Billy had had no part in pulling him away from the job that he had been sent out on and putting him on the path of the Hunsackers. But now he had run them to earth, and was determined to have them. He had been chasing the clan for years, and he vowed that before the month was many nights

2

older, he would have the bunch of them in jail. Those that weren't buried, that is.

He was United States Deputy Marshal Custis Long, called Longarm by both friend and enemy alike. The name came partly from his last name, and partly from the fact that he had made it a religion to chase his quarry to the ends of the earth if need be. He never quit on a trail, hot or cold, and he never failed to get his man. He was the long arm of the law in person, or more simply, Longarm.

He sat there, smoking, trying to think of some way to get at the Hunsackers. No immediate solution came to mind. He could see his face in the dirty window. Already he had a few days' growth on his face, and he looked tired and felt like he could use a bath. But there would be no bath in this part of the country, unless it was dust for water and tumbleweed for a towel.

His face said forty years of age, but his big arms and hands and shoulders and his quick and lithe way of moving said closer to thirty. Longarm was one of those men whose age was a mystery to everyone but themselves, and they weren't telling. He had been a U.S. deputy marshal a good deal longer than he cared to think about. He could have been a chief marshal, and Billy Vail had offered to put him up for the promotion many times, but somehow it didn't go with Longarm's idea of being a lawman. Billy Vail's job now was to sit in an office in Denver, Colorado, and send other men out to do the work. Longarm had seen Billy shrink every day he sat there. Longarm didn't want a job like that.

There had been very little conversation between himself and the Hunsackers. He had been on assignment in Virginia City, Nevada—sent there by Billy Vail to investigate the

3

murder of a state senator. It had proved to be an easy piece of work. Even though the sheriff had been corrupt, Longarm had managed to roust out the killer and get him dispatched. After that, he had, by chance, jumped seven members of the Hunsacker clan in Reno.

The Hunsackers were four brothers, the old man, and two cousins. They had fled at the sight of him, and had had a good start by the time he could get himself organized, but he had trailed them mercilessly, riding almost night and day. He had two horses, which was fortunate, and their trail had gone along a way where there was plenty of water. He had managed to kill one of the so-called cousins with a long rifle shot. After that, they had loaded up their belongings like jackrabbits and taken off.

It had surprised him when they had gone to ground in the stone mansion in the town of Lodestar, but considering the surroundings, it really wasn't a bad place to hole up. If Longarm went for help, he'd be gone for so long that they could scatter to the ends of the earth. If he simply tried to wait them out, they would win, because he didn't have the provisions or the patience to last. The one fortunate thing was the pump in the livery station that kept a big wooden tub full of water so that he was able to water his horses and himself. Otherwise, he would have to make do with what provisions he had in his saddlebags.

There was no question of attacking the place frontally. They could riddle him at least a half-dozen times before he even got thirty yards in front of the building. He sat there by the window, watching the evening get low, bringing with the lowering sun a little relief from the intense heat. The air was high and cool at night, but when the sun was cutting through it, it was like sitting on the edge of a hot skillet.

After watching for a while, Longarm ducked out of the door and skittered down to the livery stable to see about his horses. He noticed that the Hunsackers seldom fired at him, even when he was within a hundred yards, which wasn't a particularly long rifle shot. Maybe they were enjoying playing with him. He couldn't be sure. All he knew was that there were a lot of jobs that he would much rather have than the one he was presently employed in. It was taking too long, and he couldn't see any way to bring it to a satisfactory conclusion.

The Hunsackers were one of the numerous outlaw clans that populated Longarm's territory, which was generally Arizona, New Mexico, Colorado, Texas, and Nevada. It seemed as if most of these families had come West hoping to discover an El Dorado, a wealth of riches, either in the gold mines, in ranching, or in farming. When they'd realized what a hard-bitten country they were in, they'd turned to crime as a way to make their fortune. The Hunsackers were not much worse, and no better, than half-a-dozen other such outfits that Longarm had run across in the last ten years. Several he had wiped out, and several were still running at large, just like the Hunsackers.

The Hunsackers were murderers. They were thieves. They were burglars. They were train robbers. They were stagecoach robbers. They were whatever it took to get your money in their pockets. Of the Hunsacker bunch, Longarm calculated that the oldest son, LeeRoy, mostly called Lee, was the most dangerous. For pure cunning, the old man, J.J. Hunsacker, was no slouch himself. The rest were somewhere in the middle between bad and awful.

Longarm figured this band now had about ten members in all. He didn't know where the rest of them were hiding, but he had the uneasy feeling that they might be somewhere close. That would be all that he needed, to have three or five or six others come riding in to catch him unawares. He had all he could handle with the six hemmed up in the stone house. He didn't need to be caught in the cross-fire between two well-armed and well-provisioned parties of men who could shoot. As a general rule, he could deal with odds of four or five to one, but he had never cared for much higher.

Longarm settled himself in the stables, looked his two horses over with a critical eye, and saw that they were in good shape. He dug in his saddlebags and got out some cheese, dried beef, and biscuits that were rapidly becoming one day too old, and made himself the best meal he could.

In that high elevation, the sun stayed up a long time, but when it went down, it went down in a hurry. Fortunately, it seemed like the moon and the sun were balanced against each other. Once the sun was down, the moon popped up to take its place. In the clear air of that altitude, the moon put out nearly as much light as the sun, a fact that made it all that much harder to slip up on the stone house.

Longarm wondered why the mine owner who had built the house had made it so much like a fort with small windows and a heavy door. Maybe he had figured that the day would come when the miners who were making five dollars per day while he was making five thousand dollars per day would decide that it was time to turn the tables.

Longarm had not the slightest idea of how he was going to get the Hunsackers shaken loose from their hiding place. There seemed to be no way. He had only provisions for a couple more days. After that, it would mean going back to Reno or Virginia City or to Mono Lake. There was still some moldy hay in the livery stable, and his horses were making our fairly well on that, along with a couple of sacks of oats that had been left behind. But Longarm wasn't going to make out very well on the cheese that was getting harder than his teeth.

After he had eaten, he sat, smoked, and had a nip of the Maryland whiskey he tried always to carry with him. He didn't have many luxuries in his life—the odd woman here and there, and the silken taste of the whiskey. His job was such that it ought to have paid about ten thousand dollars a month, but Billy Vail couldn't seem to see it that way. Longarm drew what pay he could, and shipped what horses he could back home and tried to make a little profit on the side.

Lodestar was like a hundred other deserted towns in Nevada. Longarm had seen a good many of them. He had seen them in their flush days when storefront running footage cost forty dollars a foot, when there were ten saloons, when there was even talk about building a school, when there was even a fire department and police—all that while the mines were paying off.

Then one day, just like a water tap being cut off, it would change. Overnight, people slipped away. Overnight, the buildings were vacated. You might even walk into some of those towns and find a beer still sitting on the counter of the saloon, not a soul in sight. Lodestar was not anything extraordinary. Longarm wondered, however, if it was the headquarters of the Hunsacker clan, or if was just one of a half-dozen or so places where they knew they could hole up and give anybody a good fight.

Longarm waited until about nine o'clock, and then went out the back door of the livery stable and slipped down the backs of the line of buildings on the main street until he got to the corner. He was within twenty-five yards of the stone house now, and he could see it clearly. The rifles were still on guard.

He called out, at first softly and then with increasing volume, "LeeRoy. LeeRoy Hunsacker. Lee, it's Longarm. I want to talk."

There was a pause before a voice came back from one of the upstairs windows. "What the hell do you want, Longarm? Why don't you get on your damned horse and get out of here?"

"Listen, Lee. If you boys will surrender to me, I can guarantee to get you to jail without nobody else being killed. But I've got a party of deputy marshals on the way, and I can't guarantee you what will happen then."

Hunsacker laughed softly. "You say you've got a party of deputy marshals heading here to back you up? Is that right, Longarm?"

Longarm said, "You heard me, Lee. Now, they'll be here tomorrow or the next day, and I can't account for what an active interest they might take in this affair. There could be some thinning out of the ranks."

Hunsacker laughed again, this time out loud. He said, "Longarm, you get more full of it every day. Just exactly when did you send for this passel of deputy marshals? It would appear to me that you just barely took time to tighten the cinch on the saddle before you jumped on it and took out after us."

Longarm said, "Well, Lee, that's where you are wrong. I had plenty of time to give you all a look to see which

8

way you were heading before I ducked back into town and got off a telegram. I am telling you, Lee. You're going to get a surprise.''

"And where are they supposed to find us? I take it you gave them directions to this place here? We're forty miles from Reno, Mr. Deputy Marshal Custis Long.''

"Lee,'' Longarm said, "you're taking chances with your own life and the lives of your brothers and your daddy. Let me talk to the old man. Maybe he's got some sense.''

Hunsacker said, "No, I don't reckon, Longarm. The old man is sleeping. He don't need to be roused up by you. Now, let me give you some advice. You can't get at us. You can't even get near us. I doubt seriously that you have enough provisions, especially for your horses, to hold out very long. If you'd like to rush this place, you're more than welcome.''

Longarm said, "No, listen. You boys have done some tolerably bad business in your time, but you ain't ever shot a United States marshal. If you get into that bracket, you're liable to be plumb sorry.''

LeeRoy Hunsacker said, "Listen, Longarm. It's my turn to come off watch, and I don't feel like sitting here jawing with you. It's plain that you ain't got a card in your hand to play, so why don't you just get on out of here and leave us to be?''

"Lee, go and wake your daddy up. I know he's got more sense than you do. I'd like to talk to him.''

"I done told you, he's sleeping and he don't want to be woken up.''

"Well, it's the law saying that he ought to be woke up, so you go on in there and get him. I want to talk to him.''

There suddenly came the sound of another voice, an

older, fuller one. "Is that you, Longarm?" It was J.J. Hunsacker. "What the hell do you want? Don't you have no better sense than to come around here at this time of the night and wake people up, bothering the good at heart?"

Longarm laughed. "Well, J.J., I'd reckon that I'd have to yell mighty loud if I was going to bother anybody that was going to be described as good at heart. I don't know anybody in the immediate vicinity that could be described like that."

J.J. Hunsacker said, "Well, I reckon that you know yourself as it is." His voice faded as he turned his head. Longarm could hear the old man say, "Go on to bed, Lee. I'll take the watch for a while."

Hunsacker turned back to the window and said, "Now, here you are, Longarm, in the big middle of the Nevada desert. You ain't got no idea of where you are really, 'cause this ain't your natural stomping grounds. You're by yourself. Just what in the hell do you plan to do against the six of us? And by the way, I don't appreciate you shooting that boy yesterday."

"That boy, as you called him, one of your cousins, I think, was wanted in about ten states for everything from road agentry to bank robbery. Besides that, he was doing a pretty brisk job of shooting at *me*. You shouldn't have left him as your rear guard if he was so valuable to you."

J.J. said, sounding careless, "Well, to tell you the truth, he wasn't that much of a hand. He wasn't actually kin, you know. We just kind of took him in. Naturally, he'd be the one that we'd leave as rear guard. I was curious to see if you still had your wits about you. I thought he might catch you off center and plug you one."

"Sorry to disappoint you, J.J., but it just didn't work out

10

that way. Now listen here. Now that I am talking to the head of this outfit, what do you say to you and the balance that's left coming on out and surrendering and let's go back to Reno and get this foolishness over with real quick. You know that you can't stay in that rock house forever. Sooner or later, you've got to run out of groceries and water and whiskey and smokes.''

The old man chuckled. ''Oh, Longarm, I think it will be a long time before we run out of what you ain't got now.''

Longarm said, ''J.J., you don't know how I'm fixed. You talk mighty well for a man who ain't completely in the know about all matters. How old are you anyway, J.J.? You fifty?''

Chapter 2

Hunsacker said, "Well, I don't reckon that that'd be a damned bit of your business, Longarm. But since it's you asking, I'll tell you that I'm eight years over forty and still able to do my day's work when the time comes."

Longarm said, "J.J.,we don't call robbing banks and holding up people on the road work. Work is something you do with cattle or with goats or with a plow or a shovel. You've got it kind of confused. Taking other people's money when they ain't willing to give it to you ain't work."

J.J. Hunsacker cackled slightly. "Longarm, why don't you step out in that patch of moonlight so I can get a good look at you?"

Longarm said, "I'd be glad to, J.J., but I am afraid that with your eyesight, as old as you are getting, that you might hit me in the foot or someplace where it might hurt. The light ain't quite good enough for me to be taking any chances on your aim."

Longarm could hear Hunsacker cough and spit. Then he heard the gurgle of a bottle. "Listen, Longarm," the old man said. "Why don't you take on off and do us both a favor? I tell you what I'll do. I'll pitch five thousand dollars in gold out the front door, and you can pick it up and take it with you."

"Well, I'll be damned," Longarm said. "You mean that you're going to offer me a bribe? I've never had a bribe offered to me before, J.J. That's damned interesting of you."

Hunsacker said, "Can't you see that we've got a Mexican standoff here? You can't get at us, and we ain't going to get at you, and there's not a damned thing either of us can do about it. You ain't got no help coming. You might as well turn around and ride back to Reno and wire for some help. In the three or four days that'll take you, we can be out of here and be gone to ground someplace else, and you won't be getting your bunch into a gunfight, and nobody will be hurt, and everybody will be happy. How about that?"

Longarm said, "Well, if you don't mind, J.J., I think I'll just stick around here for a little while."

Hunsacker snorted, "Well, at least go to bed. Hell, I can't stand these all-night talks much longer. If you ain't planning on shooting us, don't talk us to death."

Without a word, Longarm stepped back along the line of empty buildings, disappearing while J.J. Hunsacker was still talking. He slipped quietly into the livery stable, checked on his two horses, and then spread out his bedroll on a mound of straw and hay he had raked up. He lay down, not bothering to take his boots off or loosen his belt. He left his revolver in the holster. Using his saddle for a

14

pillow, he put his hat over his face and settled down to sleep.

He didn't plan to sleep very much. He had taught himself over the years to take short fifteen-minute naps, and then come awake long enough to sense what was happening around him before drifting back into a light sleep. But tonight, he couldn't get quite settled. He got out his watch and looked at the time, and saw that it was nearing ten o'clock. He had a bottle of his Maryland whiskey out and near to hand. He took time to pull down a snort, cork the bottle, and then settle back again on his saddle and make-shift bed.

Longarm's mind was busy. It was a puzzle what he would do. By the time he was able to get together enough of a party to attack the stone house, it would be four or five days before they could make it back to the ghost town of Lodestar. By then, the Hunsackers would have scattered to the winds, going to any one of a dozen hideouts. Longarm didn't see any other choice but to stay here as long as he could. Maybe they weren't as well provisioned as they had bragged to him they were. Maybe they didn't have as big a supply of water. Maybe there wasn't water aplenty for their horses. He didn't know.

The best he could do would be to hang on until the very last moment. He and the horses could make it back to Reno without any fodder, and there was water along the way. When the food ran out for the horses, he would have to make a decision as to what to do, but until then, he would just keep the Hunsackers bottled up and uncomfortable. He planned to fire a few shots through the windows from time to time, just to interrupt their sleep. Truth be told, he wasn't that long on ammunition and he didn't think the game was

15

worth a candle. It might cause them a little inconvenience, but it would cause him a little more than inconvenience to run out of ammunition.

As he lay there ruminating on his latest problem, waiting for sleep to come, Longarm thought back to his last encounter with the Hunsackers, one that had come to a fight. He had not fared as well in the situation as he might have wished.

Longarm had gotten information that the Hunsackers, after several robberies in the panhandle of Texas, had fled to New Mexico and were in the Las Cruces area. He had taken the train from Denver to the area around the mining town just south of Sante Fe. The Hunsackers had been much easier to find than he had expected. There had been fourteen, more or less, holed up at the ranch house about five miles outside Las Cruces.

He had recruited several sheriff's deputies, and they had surrounded the place as much as four men could surround any place. He had called on J.J. Hunsacker to come out. When the old man had called back that he would see him in Hell first, a brisk gunfight had come about. Unfortunately, Longarm had lost one deputy who had been a little too daring—he had taken a bullet in the thigh. It had taken Longarm most of the first part of the gun battle to bind up the deputy's wounds.

After that, Longarm had been able to work his way to the back of the ranch house, and firing through a back window, he had hit several members of the gang. But then, they had rushed out to the back corral, firing as they came, and Longarm had been forced to seek cover. He had been able to kill two more as they had fled, but another deputy had gone down, and Longarm was faced with the choice

16

of chasing after J.J. Hunsacker and his family and friends or getting medical attention for the two young deputies. He had chosen to see after the deputies.

Never, at any point, had he been able to get J.J. in his gunsight. It just never seemed to happen. In the several forays he had had with the robber band, Longarm had never been able to cut the old man out and gun him down, and the same went for his favorite sons, LeeRoy and Shank and either Joe or Jack—he could never be sure of the boy's name. They were all of a similar cast, mean and rough and able to fend for themselves without much regard for other men.

It had been a close thing, getting both of the deputies back into the town to a doctor. But in the end, neither one had died. It had made Longarm even angrier toward Hunsacker and his gang. Three times he had had them under gunfire, and three times the old man had gotten away with just the loss of a few distant relatives or friends or hangers-on or whatever they were. Lying there now in the stable, Longarm gritted his teeth. Once again he had the old man dead to rights, but he still had to put him in jail or in a shallow grave in the sandy soil of Nevada.

Longarm thought on about the gunfight in New Mexico. The Hunsackers had left a young Mexican woman at the ranch when they'd fled. It had turned out that she belonged there, and had only served as a maid for the gang, who'd little time to get settled before Longarm jumped them out.

He remembered the night he spent in the ranch house after he had gotten the deputies into town. He could still see the lovely form of the Mexican woman silhouetted in the moonlight gleaming through a large window of the bedroom in the house. He guessed her to be in her early twenties. Her name was Juanita, and she burned with a fine hatred against all of the Hunsackers, LeeRoy, Shank, and the old man in particular. The Hunsackers had come into the ranch, killed the owners, and run off everyone except her. They had kept her on only to serve them. Her hatred had transferred itself into gratitude toward Longarm when he'd routed the gang.

That night, she undressed him, stood him in a tub of warm water, and slowly and carefully washed his body. After that, she took him to her bed and its clean sheets, and dried him with her kisses, working her way all up and down for as long as he would allow it. Finally, shivering and shaking with excitement, he pulled her up to him, loving the feel of her silken skin against his fingertips and his lips. He explored her soft belly with his mouth, and then moved down to the inside of her thighs.

Then, when she groaned impatiently, he thrust himself into her, and they rode and tumbled across the bed as they humped away toward the goal of a climax, their excitement building. Finally, he was no longer able to contain himself. He almost crushed her with his strong arms as the feeling that had swept through them exploded on top of the mountain. He tumbled downward, little by little, until he finally fell off and lay flat on his back, his arms outstretched, gasping for air.

That had been a good memory of the fight at the ranch. The only bad part had come when Longarm set out to try to pick up the trail of the Hunsackers and find the direction they had taken. Two men jumped up before him about a quarter of a mile from the ranch, firing as they came. He killed both, spinning one around with a bullet through the side of his chest. He killed the other a little slower with a slug through the gut. They both died, but it amazed Longarm that J.J. Hunsacker could demand such loyalty that two men would stay behind, practically giving up their lives. Longarm had no doubt that the two men had expected they could kill him, the odds being what they were. He thought probably that Hunsacker had given the men to understand that Longarm was a slouch and could be easily taken. J.J. Hunsacker was no friend, not even to his friends. Now it made Longarm shake his head as he worked toward sleep. This, he decided, was one old man who wasn't going to get away.

Longarm awoke for the last time just before dawn. It had been cold all night, and he had slept uncomfortably and chilled. His light bedroll was not up to the job of handling the desert night air. With creaking joints, he got up, looked carefully around, and then saw to his horses, doling out some grain in a feed trough for both of them. He patted the nearest animal on the rump. He was a roan gelding, sixteen and a half hands high, that Longarm had bought in Virginia City. The second horse had been an afterthought, a little bay that had surprised him with her staying power. She was gentle to a fault, but she did tend to shy and spook at the least thing.

The Hunsackers had been on his mind almost from the instant he had opened his eyes. Now, he got some of the dried beef and some of the bread, and made breakfast as best as he could. Having no coffee, he made do with some water sweetened with a little whiskey.

The taste made Longarm grimace. He turned and looked out the livery's back door toward the brilliant sunrise as it cleared the last mist of night away and heated everything it touched with its rays. It was going to be a hot day, all right.

Longarm sighed, got up, and busied himself, getting ready for the day. He needed a shave, but he was damned if he was going to go through the trouble. The Hunsackers were going to have to surrender soon, or Longarm would have to surrender to the hunger.

Longarm walked out the front door of the livery stable, casually smoking a cigarillo. The livery was at the north end of the town, with the stone house being some four hundred yards distant to the south. He turned right and walked toward it, puffing on his cigarillo and admiring the day, which had not quite reached the acme of its temperature. It was still just pleasant enough to where a man could stand it.

The first store was fifty yards toward the stone house. He walked through the dust and sand, then stepped up on the boardwalk, walking carefully so as to avoid the rotting places and the broken boards. There was a roof over the sidewalk all the way down the street, and it gave enough shade so that it was deliciously cool as he walked along. He wasn't going anywhere in particular, certainly not too near the stone house. He hadn't even brought his rifle, and he certainly didn't plan to get within pistol shot of the house.

As he walked, he looked at the stores and thought about the inhabitants when the town had been a going concern. He passed the general mercantile, and wondered how many saddles and sacks of beans and feet of rope and cans of nails the place had sold when the mines were working and people were convinced the town had a future. They had been convinced in spite of the fact that there had been thirty

20

other towns that had gone to seed ahead of them. He took a puff and blew out the blue smoke, watching it through the occasional hole in the boardwalk roof that allowed little shafts of brilliant sunlight through.

He had gone another half a block when there suddenly appeared small holes in the porch roof. He heard the high-pitched whine of bullets as they ricocheted, and then the crack of rifles being fired from somewhere up ahead. He never paused, just whirled and went through the first door he could find. The firing stopped. He squatted in the corner of a deserted cafe and cursed softly under his breath.

They had seen him come out of the livery stable, and they had seen him walk under the awning in front of the stores, and had been able to catch sight of him through the big holes in the roof. They had made a guess of where he was, and then put up a furious fusillade of rifle fire. Hell, the damned fools could have killed him. It made him furious.

Longarm found the back door out of the cafe, and then ran down the buildings toward the stone house. When he came to a corner where he couldn't be fired upon, but where he could be heard from, he let out a yell. "J.J.! J.J. Hunsacker! Come out of your hole. I want to talk to you, you sonofabitch."

After a moment, the man's mild voice came back. "That you, Longarm? What's the matter? You got a burr under your saddle blanket?"

Longarm said, "Listen, you sonofabitches. I was just walking along. I wasn't messing with you all and the next thing I know, you let out a volley of rifle fire on me. You damned idiotic sonofabitches, you could have killed me."

J.J. Hunsacker said easily, "Is that a fact, Longarm? Do

21

tell. Well, that would have been a most horrid shame."

"Listen, Hunsacker," Longarm said, "this ain't no more fun for me than it is for you. This shooting at me is going to get your ass in trouble. The best thing you can do is to come on out of that joint and go with me. The less trouble you give me, the less trouble on you. You ain't got no wanted poster notices on you for murder yet. But the day is coming, if you keep on like this, when there will be. You take my meaning?"

"Oh, I take your meaning, all right, Longarm. Did you take our meaning a while ago?"

"I took your meaning that you were trying to hit me."

"That's generally why we pop the cap on a cartridge, to hit something. Don't see no damned point in shooting to miss. But if you took our meaning, then it looks like you'll haul your freight and get the hell out of here. We ain't coming out and you ain't getting at us, so you might as well get on out."

Longarm said, "Am I bothering you all? I never recollect being so unwanted in any one place in all my life. You all don't seem to want me around. How come is that? You got someplace you need to be?"

Hunsacker said, "Hell, Longarm, you can't watch us all the time. If we wanted to slip out, we could do it when you're asleep without any trouble."

Longarm said, "I wouldn't be so damned sure of that, but I am sure you are damned anxious for me to be out of this part of the country. Makes me wonder."

"Well, you just keep on wondering. Meanwhile, I am going to have to get you to excuse me. I've got some break-fast to tend to. I've got some ham and eggs that need eating. You have any ham and eggs this morning, Longarm?"

Longarm was silent, thinking about the dried beef that he had eaten.

J.J. said again, "Why don't you come on up here and have breakfast with me, Longarm? It would be a treat to have your company."

Longarm turned away. "Go to Hell, Hunsacker. Just go to Hell."

He walked slowly back to the livery stable, his mind busy and his head full of thought. He couldn't see any clear-cut plan. He could slip around and make a try for their horses, but he reckoned that would be pretty risky. The horses were in a small corral at the back of the house, and he imagined that they were guarded by more than one rifle, night and day. No, getting at their horses was not the way. Getting at *them* was what was going to be necessary.

He stepped into the livery stable and spent an idle moment rubbing down the roan gelding with an old empty feed sack. Nothing could come to his mind about getting at the Hunsackers. The alternative was to go for help, but he knew that when he left, so would they. All he could do was to hold out as long as he could. He didn't know how long that was going to be, maybe one more day.

Because of his reputation of always running down and bringing back his man, he hated giving up on them, but he was beginning to believe that this was one of those situations where he was going to have to. Oh, sure, he could go back to Reno and wire and have a half-dozen deputy marshals or local law available in a few days, but by then there would be no catching the Hunsackers. It made him want to mash his teeth in frustration.

Finally, he got up, had a drink of whiskey, and then walked out the back of the livery stable until he had the stone house in view. He settled down on a rock and commenced to watch the house to see what kind of a routine, if any, he could figure out and make use of.

Watching the stone house made for a very slow morning, but then he really didn't have much else to do. In the afternoon, for the sake of variety, he went around the livery stable and watched from the other side. It had nothing to do with shade or being cooler, because there was no shade to be found, not anywhere, not where he could see the stone house. He reckoned a man could dig down seven or eight hundred feet and it might get a little cooler, but he didn't feel much up to the effort.

His surveillance of the Hunsacker hideout yielded very sparse results. Occasionally, he would see a flicker of a body passing one of the windows, mainly upstairs, and occasionally he would hear a dim sound, but other than that, the harvest was pretty slim.

He ate as little as he could, not so much to preserve his provisions, but to make sure he didn't completely poison himself on the beef and cheese, both of which were starting to get a kind of funny taste. The biscuits had expired. He thought of burying them and holding services, but decided that was too much trouble. He had about one day's grub left, and it was not fit to be eaten. Something was going to have to happen.

It gradually grew dim and then dark. He went into the stable, put out more grain for the horses, and made sure they had water. They seemed perfectly content with the arrangement. What was time to a horse? They certainly didn't mind the wait. He reckoned, given a choice of being in a cool livery stable or carrying his 190 pounds over the hot desert sand, he'd probably choose the livery stable too.

Longarm determined to do very little sleeping that night. He had a feeling that the Hunsackers just might try to make a break sometime before daylight. It was his belief that he had caught a tone of desperation in J.J.'s voice that morning. He thought it might mean that they were thinking about running out. If that was the case, Longarm wanted to be watching.

He determined that he would take an early nap and then be on the watch from about midnight on. He calculated that if they took off, they would do it sometime in the early morning hours when it was the coolest and they could make the most tracks. The moon would go down about two or three and it would be pretty dark, but they could still be moving along and putting distance between them and him if they were able to get clear.

Longarm determined to get to bed just as early as he could. He wanted to get about an hour or two of sleep, and then be ready to stay up the balance of the night. He made what supper he could, washing it down with the whiskey and water, and settled down to sleep, if sleep would come. He set his mind to wake himself up about midnight.

He didn't know how a man could do that, but he knew that it had always been an easy trick for him. He guessed that a man got so used to telling time by a watch that he could just feel it inside of him. Longarm had never been a man to overcomplicate his mind, or any other situation, with thinking that had nothing to do with the job at hand.

It was difficult to get to sleep so early, but finally he slept. Then shortly, or so it seemed to him, he was awake again. He had his watch lying beside him, and by a shaft of moonlight that shone through a back window, he could see that it was about ten minutes until midnight.

Longarm made no attempt to get up. It was best to rest a bit, let his body get attuned to the job at hand. What he planned to do was make a great circle in the desert and come up on the stone house from the back. He would be carrying his rifle, and he would have to take advantage of the lay of the land. It was going to be hard going through the cactus and the sand and the rocks and the greasewood. He would just have to snake along through the low places, and duck down behind the humps and the mounds, until he could get to where he would have a good vantage point to see if they were going to try to make a run.

He sat up yawning, thinking about getting up and starting the two-hour walk. He figured he would need at least that much time to make the big wide circle. As he yawned, he heard a sound. It wasn't a sound his horses would make. It wasn't the sound a stray cat would make. He distinctly heard the sound of a booted foot in the front of the stable.

He sat up, slowly drawing his revolver as he did. It seemed that he had visitors. He was just about to lean forward and look around, when some sense told him that there was a presence behind him. Longarm whirled, flinging himself to the dirt as the shotgun roared and the pellets clattered into the stable wall above his head. He whipped his revolver up, sighting toward the empty back door, but the person who had fired the shotgun was off and running by the sound of the boots striking the ground. There was still the other fellow, so Longarm didn't think he could get up and run to the back door of the stable without exposing himself to whoever was out front. He eased around the partition and tried to see through the gloom.

Somewhere near the front entrance, he saw the slightest motion, and he fired, aiming low. The only reaction was a sudden scuffling run, and Longarm saw a dark figure slip around the edge of the door and take off. After that, Longarm got to his feet, walked to the back door, and looked down along the line of the back of the buildings of the ghost town. Three or four hundred yards away, a dark form was clearing the last of the buildings and running diagonally to the stone house.

The whole scene left Longarm puzzled. They had come down to get him. Instead of simply taking off into the night, they had come down with the intention of killing him. He couldn't understand that. J.J. Hunsacker and his son, LeeRoy, were outlaws, and they were low-down and they were varmints, but they weren't stupid. You didn't kill a United States deputy marshal unless you had no other choice, and they had another choice—the choice of running. They had chosen instead to come and ambush him.

Longarm walked back into the stable, found his whiskey bottle, took a drink, and then stood by his road horse, thinking the matter over, running all the details around and around in his mind.

He couldn't for the life of him figure out what they must have been thinking. To him, it had been a damned fool play. What did they have to gain from killing a United States deputy marshal other than biting off a hell of a chaw of trouble?

Surely, they could have figured out to make a getaway. If they had to, as a last resort, they could have lain in wait for him on the trail and crippled him or his horse. There was a lot of things they could have done instead of attempting to assassinate a member of the Federal Marshals Service.

Something else was up. They wanted him gone, and it

wasn't to make a getaway. He wondered if the attack had been a bluff, if its main intention had been to scare him off. One thing for certain, they weren't going to tell him, and he doubted that he could figure it out, not even using their way of thinking. Finally, Longarm shook his head and gave it up as one problem too many, took another drink of whiskey, and then with his carbine in his hand, went out into the street to see what was transpiring down at the other end of the street where the stone house stood.

He walked about halfway down until he was about two hundred yards from the house, then casually threw six shots through the upstairs windows. Even before the echo of the shots had died, he could hear a considerable amount of yelling and excitement. It made him smile. If they weren't going to allow him to sleep, he didn't see any reason to let them have their peace either. When some of the commotion had died down, he yelled out, "J.J., that's just a little of what you're going to get in the next few days! I've got six deputies on their way!"

He waited a few moments for a reply, but when none was forthcoming, he turned and trudged back to the livery stable and into the gloom of the back. He was well and truly puzzled. It was unlike anything he knew about their past history. They were sneaks rather than folks who would confront you and take you on in a fight. Longarm took a moment to light a cigarillo, and then he sat down on a couple of sacks of aging feed, smoking, thinking, and trying to figure this situation out.

One thing was certain. The attack didn't change his plans. As bad as he dreaded the idea of footing it in a long circle around the stone house, he didn't really see any way of getting out of it. If anything, their midnight visit made it all that much more important that he take a scout and see just exactly how they were situated. It wasn't pleasant now, and it wasn't going to be pleasant. But then, as Billy Vail would say, if it was so damned much fun being a deputy marshal, they wouldn't bother to pay you. Well, he could always reply to Billy Vail that he, Longarm, made more money playing poker and trading horses than he ever did getting paid by the United States Government for wearing a little tin badge around.

Longarm faced the fact that he would have to leave and make the trek. He checked his rifle, and then put a dozen extra .44-caliber cartridges in the pockets of his jeans and his shirt. After that, he went out the back entrance to the stable, leaving his horses to get along as best as they could. It was about 1:15 by his watch when he left.

Chapter 3

The going was rougher than he had imagined. The sand was loose, and there were thousands of little rocks and stones and cactus plants every ten feet or so that pronged him as he stepped. He hadn't gone a hundred yards away from the livery stable before he had stuck a cactus thorn through his jeans and into his calf. It hurt so bad, he nearly cursed out loud. As it was, it was tough going to keep himself concealed from the stone house. If anyone had been on careful guard, he imagined they would have already seen him. But he had gotten a break. It was a dark night, clouds shadowing what moonlight there was in the desert.

He headed almost due west for five or six hundred yards, before he turned back toward the south to go past the house and come up from behind it. The loose sand was the biggest irritant. After a half mile, his legs were so tired from the work required to walk through the nasty stuff, he wasn't sure he could make it. If he hit a soft spot, his boot would sink halfway into what was supposed to be firm ground.

He cursed under his breath most of the first part of the trip. The second part, he didn't have the breath to curse.

He ran across a small gallery of scrub brush, mostly greasewood with some mesquite mixed in. With that as a cover, he was able to stoop down and make some time.

There was only one window on the west side of the house. It was dark, but he still kept his eye on it looking for any signs of movement. Finally, he was beyond the house and could start curving back to the east so that he could see what was happening at the back. If they were going to leave and try to lose him, they had to get their horses from the back.

From a position about a mile south of the stone house, Longarm worked his way forward, moving from one clump of mesquite to a high place in the ground to a gully, and then to any other kind of cover he could find to keep himself well hidden. He was approximately six hundred yards short of the house when he went to ground in a little gully, stretching his rifle out before him. He got out his watch and by the moon's dim glow, he was able to see that it was 2:30. It had taken him about an hour and fifteen minutes to come not much more than two miles—a long two miles. For a man who didn't make a habit out of walking, it was a damned long two miles. While he waited, he took his time, pulling both boots off and pouring out the sand. He couldn't figure how sand could get by his jeans, which covered the tops of his boots, and then get down inside his boots, but he reckoned there was a coffee cup full of sand in each one.

He watched the house, and nothing happened. He was close enough that he could see the Hunsacker horses distinctly. There were ten of them. He reckoned that four of them had been used as packhorses or maybe just extra mounts. Several of the horses were sleeping, standing up, one hind foot cocked and lifted off the ground and then let back down just on the toe of the hoof. You could always tell when a horse was sleeping because his tail was still. Never mind that his head was down. Most horses did that a lot of the time, but their tails were seldom still unless they were asleep.

Longarm grew restless. It was 3:30, starting toward four. There still hadn't been a sign of movement from the house. If they were going to be leaving, they were taking their own good time about it. Perhaps, he thought, they might have spotted him.

Yet there had been no disturbance, no sign of movement from the house. It had been as still as a graveyard. At four, he stirred and raised up slightly. There didn't seem to be much point in waiting much longer. He crawled out of the gully and then began working his way backwards a few hundred yards before he found the kind of cover he wanted. Once he headed west, he took it slow, watching the house and the horses, listening for any movement. Finally, he came even with the west side of the house again, and paused to look the situation over. He was in a clump of mesquite and greasewood, and it was a good a place to take a rest. His watch said it was near five o'clock, and there was still no movement from the house.

After a short break, Longarm pushed on north, hurrying a little because it was coming dawn and he didn't want to be caught out in the desert on foot just in case the Hunsackers were watching for him.

The growth of greasewood and mesquite ran almost a thousand yards, and he made good use of it. His legs were tired from lumbering through the loose sand, and he paused to rest every so often. It didn't really matter because by now, he was out of rifle range and there would damned little they could do about it even if they did catch sight of him. He was nearly even with the livery stable, but he was still some six or seven hundred yards to the west of it. He paused at the last of the mesquite and sagebrush to kneel down on one knee and take a rest. He was damned if his job involved walking four miles in one night in high-heeled boots in loose sand that was full of rocks and cactus and probably a whole lot of crawling things he didn't want to run into.

Toward the east, he could see a faint glow in the sky that told him the sun was rising. It hadn't nudged its way over the horizon yet, but it was fast coming. He yawned, got out a cigarillo, and lit it. While he smoked, he looked toward the northwest, toward the open country that led to the foothills of the mountains. He was surprised that the Hunsackers hadn't held up in there. That was their natural habitat. It was full of all kinds of hidey-holes and gullies and blind canyons where a man could get lost for a thousand years. As he was looking, he thought he saw movement in that direction. He strained his eyes, but whatever it was had gone to ground.

He was about to turn his attention to the stone house for the last time when, out of the corner of his eye, he caught the movement again. He whipped his head around and stared long and hard. Yes, it was definitely something moving across the desert. It was a good ways off, maybe four or five miles, maybe more. It was difficult to tell in the clear, still mountain air, but he could tell that it wasn't a mounted rider. It was too big. As it came on, he was finally able to distinguish that it was a mule-drawn buggy. At least, that was what the brief glances he got of it made him think. It disappeared from time to time as it hit low spots in the desert or ran behind a rise.

Now he turned and watched it intently. It seemed to be moving at a pretty good pace. Whoever was in the buggy, if it was indeed a buggy, was interested in getting to where they were going before the sun got up and too hot. As near as he could figure, and he knew it was still too early to be making such calculations, the contraption seemed to be heading toward the town of Lodestar. He wondered if the sheriff at Reno or some deputy had become curious about him and had come to see after his welfare. But no, he thought. That couldn't be. The buggy was coming from a direction well to the west of Reno. In fact, it was coming out of the mountains.

It came on, and now he could tell that it was a buggy being pulled by something that didn't look exactly like a horse, so he assumed it was a mule. Mules were used to the desert country. A mule could go longer without water or feed. They were tougher than horses. Also, their hooves were softer and splayed out to where they could get a better grip in the sand and soft going.

Knowing it was a mule didn't answer any of the several questions that were in his mind, the main one being who was in the buggy and what they were doing headed for such a spot as Lodestar. The only people in Lodestar were him and the Hunsackers, and he doubted very seriously that whoever was driving the buggy was looking for him. That meant that whoever was coming had to be an ally of his quarry in the stone house. It behooved him to keep them from joining up with the old man and LeeRoy and the rest of the clan.

Longarm started moving westward in a line to intercept the route of the mule and the buggy. For several hundred yards, there was the cover of the bramble of the mesquite and greasewood, and he moved from clump to clump, moving as slow as he could, yet at the same time making certain that he'd be in a position to intercept the path of the buggy. He could not quite make out the passengers, but he could see that the mule wanted to get to wherever they were going before it got hotter. Mules were smart that way.

He had moved some 150 yards west when he knelt to watch the buggy. Now, it was no more than a mile away. He studied the passengers, and had a difficult time coming to a conclusion. They looked too colorful for members of the Hunsacker gang, and they weren't exactly wearing the kind of hats that most gunmen and cowboys and road agents wore in this part of the country.

He moved as quickly as he could through the bramble of bushes for another hundred yards. The buggy was now less than three quarters of a mile away. This time, as Longarm studied it, a startling thought occurred to him. There were three people in the buggy, and it appeared that they were women. He couldn't for the life of him figure out what three women would be doing flying across the desert floor at five-thirty in the morning, unless they were three of the Hunsacker men who'd decided to wear dresses for disguise.

Longarm moved west rapidly. For certain, he intended to stop the buggy. With it less than a half mile away, he could see that there were women on the seat of the buggy. He couldn't make out their features, but he could tell that two of them had long blond hair and the one in the middle, who was driving, had short, raven-black hair. It made him lick his lips unconsciously. He was hungry for a woman.

He had just gotten to know a female faro dealer in Reno when he'd run across the Hunsackers. In fact, he had been planning on inviting her for some very pleasant lovemaking the night he had taken out chasing the Hunsackers. He'd regretted more than just the loss of the woman's soft body. As far as he was concerned, faro was the worst odds a gambler could get, and yet he had sat there for several nights in a row, losing at a sucker's game while he smoothly let the good-looking woman dealer get to know him. He reckoned that she had gotten to know his money a good deal better than she had gotten to know *him*.

He crouched behind the mesquite bush and watched the buggy as it neared, steering straight as an arrow for the stone house. He itched mightily for the pair of binoculars that were, right then, back in his saddlebags. He hadn't taken them with him when he had gone to trek around the stone house because they weren't much good at night. Now it was daylight, and he wished he could see what type of ladies were occupying the buggy. He wondered if they were kin to each other, or if they were kin to the Hunsackers, or just what their relationship was to the whole matter. He doubted that they were new cooks hired to come out.

The buggy was less than a half mile away. He was going to have to do something. What, he was not certain, but the one sure thing he could do to stop them was to kill the mule. He hated to do that. It seemed like a good animal, and he had never been one to shoot horses, mules, donkeys, or any animals that you couldn't rightly eat, although he had eaten horseflesh a time or two when there wasn't anything else.

Longarm began moving, trying his best to intersect the line the buggy was making as it headed south and toward the stone house. He would be out of cover before he reached that line. Whatever he did, he was going to have to do it at comparatively long range. After fifty yards more, he was at the end of the mesquite and greasewood clump, and the only other thing that was in front of him was a broad expanse of clear sand. Clear, that is, except for small rocks and cactus.

The buggy was coming on at a fast pace. It was less than two hundred yards away. Longarm had no time to debate any longer. He put his rifle to his shoulder, pulling back the hammer with his thumb as he did. He aimed a little above and in front of the mule and fired.

Longarm saw the mule shy slightly and the women jump. The mule had spooked at the sound of the bullet as it whistled right over his head, and the women were surprised by the noise of the rifle when it reached them. But for all the good it did, he might as well have saved the bullet. The mule once again picked up his rapid trotting pace, and other than looking around, the women paid no more attention. As quickly as he could, Longarm jacked another shell into the chamber. This time, he fired the bullet right across the mule's face. The mule stopped and reared up. The women, he could see, were frightened and nervous.

He heard the black-haired one cry out shrilly, "J.J.! J.J. Hunsacker! Is that you, dammit?"

The women were no more than fifty yards away. Longarm stepped out of the clump of mesquite and started toward them, his rifle at the ready. The black-haired woman picked up the reins she had dropped when the mule had reared up. She made as if to slap the still-nervous animal on the back.

Longarm yelled out, "Hold it, lady!" He put the rifle to his shoulder. "You hit that animal and get him going, he'll be a dead animal!"

All three of the women were looking at Longarm. He was within forty yards. Already he could see that the black-haired one was older, and the two blond women were in their mid-twenties, he guessed. He walked steadfastly forward. He said, "Don't move a muscle. Drop those reins. Do it, lady! I am a United States deputy marshal, and I will use this gun if I have to."

The black-haired woman glared at him. The other two just looked interested and sort of innocent. From somewhere behind him, he heard a dim clamor and clatter and shouting and the sound of rifle fire. He turned and looked back toward the stone house. In the windows of the upper story, he could make out the dim figures of several people who appeared to be waving their arms and yelling. Now and again, one fired a rifle. He wasn't too much worried about the rifle fire, for unless they had a Sharps buffalo gun or something similar, they were well out of range of the Winchester carbines that they most likely had in their possession.

Longarm walked up to the buggy and reached out, taking the reins out of the woman's hand. He could see now that she was forty or so. The girls—he began to think of them as that—next to the hard-faced, old battle-ax that had been doing the driving, were even younger than he had thought at first.

It was a two-seater buggy, a carriage really, and he bade the two young women to get in the backseat. He said,

"Now, if anybody's got a weapon on them, a pistol, a derringer, a knife, or even a long hat pin, this is the time to declare it. If you try to use it on me, you're going to get yourself dead."

The dark-haired woman said sullenly, "You say that you are a United States marshal? Well, anybody could say that. For all me and the girls know, you're some crazy man out here in the desert."

Longarm reached in his shirt pocket, took out his badge, and held it in his palm long enough for them all to see it.

He said, "I am a United States deputy marshal and I am hunting the Hunsackers. I have them run to ground in that stone house over yonder. I have a feeling that you were going to see them."

The dark-haired woman stared resolutely out across the desert. She said, "You can go to Hell. I don't like any law, and I sure as hell don't like the kind of law you represent."

Longarm said, "Well, slide over in that seat, lady. I'll be doing the driving now."

Longarm had to half-shove her over as he stepped up into the buggy and took the reins. Turning back so he could see the two blondes, he said, "You just stay back in your seats. Don't lean forward. Don't talk. Don't yell. Don't do nothing."

They didn't answer, and he wheeled the mule to the left and started directly toward the livery stables, which were some six or seven hundred yards across the desert. As he drove, he glanced over at the stone house. He could see that the outlaws were jumping around, waving their arms, and apparently not enjoying the sight of him in charge of the buggy and its passengers. His one worry was that they might suddenly get all braved up and mount their horses and charge him before he could get inside and fort up in the livery stable. But if they did, they couldn't fire at him without endangering the women, and from the way they were acting, he didn't think they wanted to do that. In fact, the more his mind toyed with it, the more he was convinced that the women might have been the best thing that had happened to him in the whole scheme of things.

He headed more to the north, intending to circle around and come up the street and into the livery stable through the front, since there was no room to come in the back way by buggy.

Longarm watched carefully to see what was transpiring with the Hunsackers, half expecting at any moment to see four or five horsemen come bursting around the big house with rifles in their hands. By then, he was sweeping around the north line of vacant buildings. The Hunsackers had made no move. He checked the mule, who was stepping along briskly, slowed him down to a walk, and then turned into the livery stable. He knew quite well that the Hunsackers were watching his every move.

He went through the big double doors of the stable, and pulled the mule up smartly before he could get into the back of the building. Longarm jumped down and tied the reins to a post. He turned around and looked at the three women. The two blondes looked back at him solemnly, but the black-haired woman had a furious look on her face.

She said, "By damn you, sir. What right do you have to stop us on our right and lawful and peaceful business? Just who the hell do you think you are?"

Longarm stood there, looking at them, his hands on his hips for a long moment. Finally, he spat, "I've already told you who I am and what my business is. Now, you all get

41

down from that buggy. We're going to go into that office and everybody is going to take a chair and we are going to talk. Only this time, I'll be asking the questions, finding out about your business.''

For a moment, nothing happened. Longarm decided he better set the tone of the business so there would be no misunderstandings. He took a long stride to the buggy, reached in with his right arm, and got the black-haired, hatchet-faced woman by the arm, dragging her out of the buggy. He would have dragged her to the ground if she hadn't jerked back just enough to slip his grip. He was about to reach for her again when she waved him away.

"Hold on," she said. "There ain't no use throwing me on the ground. I'll get down by myself."

After that, the two yellow-haired girls followed suit, coming out immediately, stepping on the running board and then to the ground. He herded them toward the office, keeping an eye toward the street in case company came calling. The office was a fair size, and had glass on three sides, which gave him a good view to keep watch. He took a chair, and put his back to the stable part of the livery. He appointed the black-haired woman to sit behind the desk, and then let the two young women find chairs for themselves.

Longarm turned to the black-haired woman. "What's your name?"

She was dressed in a high-necked gown made from some paisley print, with a brooch at her throat collar that gathered the material up into a becoming choker. He thought to himself that she wasn't all that bad-looking, except when she was furious, which was the only view he had really had of her.

Longarm said, "What is your name, ma'am? I'm not likely to ask you many more times."

She said, "I'm Mrs. Minnie Sewell, if it's any of your business."

Longarm glanced at the woman. "Is that Mrs. or Madam?"

The woman gave Longarm an outraged look. She said, "How dare you, sir! The late Mr. Sewell would rise to mark right promptly and you would not be bully-ragging a poor helpless woman like me!"

Longarm smiled. He nodded his head at the two young women. "And who are these? Your daughters?"

Mrs. Sewell said, "Well, now, Marshal. I'm certain they can tell you if they are of a mind to give you their names."

Longarm turned toward the two young women. They were sitting quite calmly, composed. The first one had a green ribbon in her hair that went very well with her coloring. He could see that she had used a little rouge on her cheeks and on her lips. He said, "What's your name, miss?"

She cocked her head, gave him a slight smile, and said, "My name? What do you want with my name? Men don't usually want my name. That's not what they're after. They want something other than my name."

Longarm looked at her for a long moment, thinking how right she was. He could feel the swelling rising in his groin just looking at her. She was right. It would be a damned fool of a man who would only want her name. He said, "Well, that's true, but for the time being, let's just pretend that's all I want."

"My name is Marianne Parsons, if it's any of your business," she said.

Longarm nodded. "All right, Miss Parsons. Thank you."

He looked over at the other young lady. She was not as flirtatious. She looked calm, but she also looked serious. Her yellow dress went very well with her wheat-colored hair. He could see now that they were different-colored blondes. Marianne Parsons had the lighter hair. This one's hair had a touch of brunette in it. He said, "I need to know your name, miss."

The woman looked over at Marianne Parsons, and then at Minnie Sewell, and then back at Longarm. She said in a cool, haughty voice, "I'm not certain that I care what you want, Marshal, if that's really what you are. But if you must know my name, it's Verlene Thomas."

Longarm nodded again. "That's fine. Actually, I didn't need to know any of your names. I don't really care what they are, but what I do care about and what I intend to find out is what brought you to this ghost town of Lodestar."

Longarm looked around swiftly at Minnie Sewell. He said, "I think that's the one you can answer, Mrs. Sewell. You were the one driving that mule. You knew what you were doing, where you were going. Let's have an answer."

Minnie Sewell folded her arms across her ample breast. Her face was set and her eyes piercing. "Listen here, Marshal," she said. "There are things that you ain't got the right to make me do. We ain't done nothing wrong. We ain't committed no crime and you can't say that we did. This is a free country. Where we were going and what we were going for is none of your damned business. So you just get that straight in your mind and me and you will get along just fine."

Longarm looked steadily at the woman. "Mrs. Sewell, I

have it in my mind that you are engaged in the business of prostitution.''

She opened her mouth to speak, but he put his hand up to stop her. ''Save your breath until I am done talking,'' he said. ''Maybe then you'll understand what I am trying to say. I have it in my mind that you have brought these two young ladies out here for the purpose of prostitution. That is illegal in every state and territory under the federal flag, and Nevada happens to fill that bill. So you might think that you haven't committed a crime or done any harm, but you'd be up the wrong tree, Mrs. Sewell.''

Her dark eyes had gotten even harder. ''You can just go to Hell, Marshal.''

''Deputy Marshal. You can address me as Deputy Long. The name is Deputy Custis Long. You didn't ask, but I am offering it to you in case you want to get my attention. That's the way you would do it.''

Mrs. Sewell said, ''I'd just be happy if I never heard your name again. In fact, I wish I had never set eyes on you. I said we were going about our business in a free and American way and you ain't got no right to interfere. As for this business about prostitution, you can't prove nothing. And secondly, prostitution is just as freely practiced in the territory of Nevada as it is everywhere else. Where you get off saying it is against the law is more than I can figure.''

Longarm nodded. ''I will agree with you that it is a law that is not often enforced. It's not a popular law, and it is probably only enforced in one or two states in the Northeast, but that doesn't keep it from being a law, and that doesn't keep me from enforcing it as an officer of the law any time I feel like it. And it just so happens that I feel like it right now. Do you want to tell me what you were doing, where you were coming from, and who you are heading towards? I think I already know all the answers, but I would just like to hear you say them."

Minnie Sewell said, "Did I remember to tell you to go to Hell? If not, go to Hell."

Longarm swung his eyes to the two very pretty young women sitting in the room. He said, "I have the feeling that you two are the prize that goes with the ribbon. Now, Mrs. Sewell is not going to have anybody laying awake nights waiting on her. But I do believe that you, Marianne, and you, Verlene, could set the heart racing fast in some young men that I happen to know. Now, is it true that you were coming to this town for the purpose of prostitution?"

He was looking at Verlene when he said that. She turned and looked at Marianne and gave her head the slightest shake. Longarm caught the motion. He said, "Marianne, one of you is going to tell the whole story about why you decided to drive out from Reno on a forty-mile jaunt. Someone is going to tell me the truth of this matter before it's all over. Now, it could be you, Marianne. Or it could be you, Mrs. Sewell. Or it could even be you, Verlene. You can make it hard or you can make it easy, but it's going to happen."

Marianne suddenly blurted out, "We didn't come from Reno. We didn't come from more than ten miles away."

Longarm smiled. "All right, that's a good start. Now, where was this someplace not more than ten miles away?"

Minnie Sewell said suddenly, "Marianne, you shut your mouth. I'll come over there and slap some sense into you if you're not careful."

Longarm got up. He said, "You all stay still and I'll be

46

right back. You can't make it out that door into any place before I could run you down. Be assured of that."

He went out the office door, and then cut quickly back into the stable, going past the mule and the buggy. His saddlebags were hanging over a stall partition. He rummaged inside the left pouch, and came out with two sets of handcuffs. He put one set in his rear pocket, and then went back inside the office carrying the other one.

Before the woman could realize what was happening, he had snapped one of the cuffs over the wrist of Minnie Sewell and then dragged her to her feet and around the desk. She was out the door before she realized what was happening. As he took her toward the back, she tried to kick and slap at him with her free hand, all the while directing a torrent of abuse and cuss words at him. He paid her no mind. At the first post, he found where the jaw of the loose cuff would go around, snapped it closed, and left her anchored to part of the woodwork of the livery stable. He said, "Now, the only way you'll get loose is to pull that post down, and then if you do, the roof is going to fall down on your head."

She said furiously, "If I thought, by damned, that it would get you too, I'd be willing to take the chance."

Longarm nodded and walked back into office. The two young women had been whispering between themselves, but they fell silent as he entered. He said, "All right, now we are going to get down to some truth here." He reached into his back pocket, took out the other set of handcuffs, and then said, "Or else we're going to put these to use, and then there won't be but one of you loose. And that one is going to be worked on proper. So, you can do it however you want to. Now, who wants to start telling me what you all are doing here and why and how all this stuff got made up? Who wants to go first? You, Marianne? Why don't you start?''

Chapter 4

Marianne gave Verlene a frightened look. It was clear to Longarm by now that Marianne was the more vulnerable of the two girls. Verlene was older and more experienced. It would be against Marianne that the best pressure could be applied. Longarm hated to come down hard on the pretty young woman, especially considering how long he had been out in the desert, but he felt that he had to do just that. He didn't know what purpose these women had for coming to Lodestar, whether they had been sent for by J.J. Hunsacker, or had come on their own, or just what the situation was. For all he knew they could be kinfolk to the Hunsackers. They might be engaged to some of the men. But to Longarm, they were bargaining chips to play off against the Hunsackers, and with the odds being what they were, he needed all the help he could get. He stood up, walked over, and stood near Marianne, forcing her to look up at him. Her lips were trembling, and she was blinking her eyes rapidly.

He said, "Now, listen to me, little lady. You've got yourself in over your head. You are fooling with the wrong folks. You've got yourself caught between some outlaws and the law. If you've got any sense, you'll cooperate with the law."

Marianne's lower lip started to tremble more, and Longarm saw tears start in her eyes. She made a moaning sound, and looked toward Verlene again.

The older girl said harshly, "Oh, leave her alone. If you have to bully her so, why don't you come ask me?"

At that moment, the progress between them was interrupted by yelling and cursing from the interior of the stable. Minnie Sewell was making sure she was not being forgotten. Longarm gave the two women a look and said, "Don't either of you make a move." With that, he turned on his heel and walked out into the stable, untying the handkerchief from around his neck as he walked.

Minnie Sewell was in fine voice. She stopped when she saw him, but just for an instant. In the next, she let out a long string of curses. Longarm caught her with her mouth wide open, and jammed the handkerchief in and tied it around behind her mouth so that she was gagged but not bound. She could reach up and free the gag with the hand that was not handcuffed, so Longarm was forced to get out his key, unlock the cuff that was around the post, then force Minnie Sewell over to where he could get both of her arms around the post, and then click the jaw of the free handcuff onto her other wrist. She was much more uncomfortable now, but at least she couldn't pull the handkerchief loose.

Longarm said, "I hope you are satisfied. You've managed to get yourself into a very handy position. Let's see what you can do now. You had better hope that the Hunsackers don't go to shooting through the roof again. There's a damned good chance they'll hit you. You're just about in the middle.''

She gave Longarm a look with wide, frightened eyes. She struggled to push the gag out of her mouth with her tongue, but wasn't successful. Longarm turned and walked into the office.

Verlene said before he could even ask her, ''Well, if you have to know, Marianne and I are suppose to marry two of the Hunsacker family.''

Longarm stared at her in disbelief. ''Marry? You mean with a preacher or a justice of the peace?''

Marianne started to speak, but Verlene stared straight back at Longarm. She said, ''I know you think we are whores, and maybe we have been, but a deal was made through Mrs. Sewell and we are to marry two of the Hunsacker boys. It's going to be a marriage, proper and legal, and you can think what you want to about it. But you've got no right to hold us, no right to keep us from going to men we are engaged to marry.''

Longarm smiled slowly. It was even better than he had hoped. He'd thought that he had intercepted some whores that J.J. Hunsacker had hired to keep his stud horses in line. He couldn't believe that he had intercepted a bridal party. He said, ''What about Minnie Sewell? Who was she going to marry? Old J.J. himself?''

Verlene folded her arms and looked out the front window. She said, ''Whatever Mrs. Sewell's business is, it's none of mine and I doubt that it's any of yours.''

Longarm said, ''Next you'll be telling me that she didn't own the whorehouse that you worked at.''

Verlene gave him a look. ''Next, I won't be telling you

51

anything. Next, we'll be getting up and walking out of this office and going down to where we are supposed to be right now.''

Longarm slowly took the extra pair of handcuffs out of his pocket and said, "I don't think you'll be going anywhere to see anybody."

Marianne said, "I wish we had never come. I wish we were home and it was all over with."

Verlene gave her a hard look. "Be quiet, Marianne."

Longarm said, "And just where is home? Where did you all come from? You say you didn't come from Reno? Where did you come from?"

Marianne suddenly said, "There's a little town about ten miles northwest of here where a mine is still working. There's a saloon and a whorehouse there. We were working there because it's got less competition than Reno and the money was better. Even the men were more grateful, if you understand what I mean."

Longarm nodded. "Oh, I understand what you mean."

Verlene said, "What do you plan to do with us? Not that you have right to do anything."

Longarm scratched the back of his head. "Well, Verlene, I haven't exactly worked all that out in my mind yet. I've got to figure out some way to get some contact with the Hunsackers and see what they want to do about this business—see what they have to trade. I can assure you of one thing—I ain't allowing you to parade up the street and finish up getting married to a couple of them boys that I plan to see hung before the week is out. So you can put that thought right out of your mind.

"As to what I am going to do, that I cannot say. First, I know I am going to have to secure you two so that you

52

can't get to bouncing around and get loose. I don't need to be watching you every second of the time."

Marianne said, "Oh, you're not going to lock us up? Or chain us? Or tie us up? I couldn't stand that."

Longarm said, "Whatever I do, I'll see to it that you can handle it. I know that, right about now, both of you think that I am about the meanest man in the country, but that ain't necessarily the case. I ain't interested in putting a hardship on you that I don't have to. My interest is in those six or seven fellows down at the end of the street. By the way . . ." He switched his eyes over to Verlene. "Which ones were you and Marianne suppose to marry?"

Verlene seemed somewhere between disinterested and angry. "What does it matter?" she said. "Is it really any of your business? I understand that you want to put those men in jail. We were simply going to marry them."

Longarm started to say, "Sounds about like the same to me," but he caught himself in time. Instead he said, "Well, I reckon you can pretty well figure that the marriage ain't going to come off. I hope that you got some money on the deal already so that you won't hold it against me for interrupting the upcoming nuptials."

Verlene said steadily, "Whatever we got is our business. It's not yours."

Longarm said, "I am a little curious about one thing. You were coming here to marry a couple of these Hunsacker boys. Who was going to do the marrying? As far as I know, outside of me, there ain't another soul alive in this town. Who was going to be the preacher?"

Verlene drew herself up. She said, "Mrs. Sewell, for your information, is a licensed minister."

Longarm looked at her, blinking for a second. Then he

smiled slowly. "Oh, yeah," he said. "I'll just bet she is. I'd hate to find out which church, though. I'm pretty sure Mrs. Sewell is not going to be mistaken very often for a minister."

Verlene said, "Well, Marshal Long, you may or may not know everything. It appears that you think you do, but in this case, you just happen to be wrong. I have seen her diploma on the wall of her house. So there."

Longarm was about to speak when he heard the sound of a voice shouting from somewhere up the street. He jumped to his feet and ran to the big double doors of the stables. He could distinctly hear someone shouting now. With a cautious left eye, he peered out the door, looking up the street toward the big house. He could see three figures walking down the middle of the street. At times, one of them called out his name, and at other times, all three of the men called out, "Longarm! Longarm! Show yourself! We've got business to talk!"

The only one of them that Longarm recognized was LeeRoy. He was the one carrying the white flag. It was nothing more than what appeared to be a torn-up sheet tied to a slim piece of wood. Longarm slid his carbine around the edge of the door and dropped to one knee. He steadied his sight on LeeRoy, who was in the middle. He called out, "That'll do you right there. That's far enough. You can stop right there."

The men came to a halt. LeeRoy Hunsacker said, "That you, Longarm?"

Longarm said, "Were you expecting someone else?"

"We need to talk."

"What do you want to talk about?"

One of the other men spoke. He appeared younger and

54

lighter-haired than LeeRoy, but Longarm didn't know his name. He said, "It's about those women you took. They were supposed to be our brides."

Longarm said, "What's your name?"

The young man said, "Joe. Joe Hunsacker, and you have my bride in there."

LeeRoy said, "And you have mine too, Longarm. They ain't got nothing to do with the law, and you ought to turn them loose. You ain't got no business holding them there, and you have that Mrs. Sewell. She's a nice lady."

Longarm said, "Well, LeeRoy, you ain't got much to trade. I can see now, though, why you wanted me out of this town. You wanted me out of here before these ladies showed up. Well, it's a little late for that now. I've got the ladies, and you can have my share of the stale cornbread. I am about to get impatient with you and this carbine. So, just start walking backwards. The next time I see you, there is not going to be any talk of truce. Do you understand?"

The other two started backing away, but LeeRoy held his ground. He said, his voice almost in a wail, "What am I supposed to tell Daddy? What kind of a deal will you come to on this matter?"

Longarm said, "I don't know, but we ain't reached it yet. Make sure that Daddy understands that nobody else better offer me any money. That's a very unhealthy occupation."

LeeRoy Hunsacker shrugged his shoulders, turned, and started walking back up the street toward the big house. After ten yards, he turned and said, "Longarm, are them girls all right?"

Longarm chuckled. "Well, they ain't got anything to eat."

LeeRoy Hunsacker said, "You mean *you* ain't got nothing to eat."

"Well," Longarm said, "if I ain't got nothing to eat, that sure as hell means those girls have nothing to eat, now don't it, LeeRoy? Why don't you get on back to J.J. and tell him that the next time he wants to talk to me, don't send three fools but get himself up and we'll make a deal."

LeeRoy said, "Are you telling me that you will deal, Marshal?"

"Yeah, I'll deal if the proposition is right. Now, get on back and tell him that. But I want it understood right now, right clear so that you don't make a mistake. There ain't going to be another flag of truce. Anybody that comes waltzing down the middle of the street, waving a bedsheet, is going to catch one right where it will do him the worst good. You had better have your hands over your head the next time you give me a sight of you. Otherwise, I'll be shooting to finish the party. Now, get on back to your daddy and tell him to work out what he wants and what he is willing to give up. And I ain't going to be satisfied with just a little helping."

Longarm watched as the three men backed off a few steps, and then turned and walked off down the street toward the big stone house. Longarm knew his own position was weak. He had to get out while his horses were still strong enough to make the forty-mile trip back to Reno.

Thinking that made him remember where the women had come from. Ten miles, one of them had said, from the northwest. He didn't know of any town there, but she'd said it was just a digging. Some miners probably prospecting on a cold strike, maybe potlucking it, digging holes in the hillside and hoping to strike a ledge or a vein or a glory hole. Certainly there was no water, so it wasn't a placer mine. It was Marianne who had told him that they had picked the place because there was no competition. Well, he supposed that was as good a reason as any. He certainly had no competition from any law officers in this wonderful town of Lodestar.

Longarm got up, turned, and walked back to the livery office. As he did, he looked at Minnie Sewell. She didn't look particularly happy with her hands handcuffed around the post and a handkerchief in her mouth. She gave him as vicious a look as he reckoned he had ever received in his life.

He said, "Mrs. Sewell, I hope you are comfortable. Lord knows I have done everything to make you so."

She kicked out at him with her foot, stirring dust up from the floor of the stable.

He went in the office. The two young women were still sitting exactly as they had been when he'd left. He could tell they hadn't come very far by the freshness of their clothes. Both of them were wearing gaily colored dresses with low-cut bodices that revealed a great deal of cream-colored skin. It caused a stirring inside him, and brought that swelling he knew so well but had no intention of doing anything about. The women were prisoners of his. For all intents and purposes, they were accomplices of the Hunsackers, and they were hostages to be bartered.

He nodded at the two young women as he came through the door, and then went directly and sat in the chair behind the desk. They stared at him openly, but neither spoke.

He stared back just as openly. "One thing has got me confused, ladies."

Verlene said, "And what would that be, Marshal?"

"I am a deputy, as you well know, so quit calling me Marshal. You're doing it on purpose."

"Yeah, Marshal," she said.

Longarm shook his head and gave her a look. "What's got me confused is that you said that you had gone to the mining camp to avoid the competition. As easy on the eye as you two are, I don't see how you would have given much of a damn abut the competition in Reno or wherever it was that you were running from."

Verlene said evenly, with nothing in her voice, "It wasn't the quality of the competition so much, Marshal, as it was the quantity. In a crowd, it's hard to pick out the prettiest face, just like it's difficult to pick out one cow in a herd. We went where the living was much easier."

Longarm nodded. "Yeah, I can understand that. Makes sense to me."

Just then, Marianne spoke up. "Dammit, Marshal or Deputy, whatever you are. I'm hungry. When are we going to have something to eat?"

Longarm looked around at her, enjoying the bright sunshiny look of her face, and the body enclosed in the tight-waisted frock she was wearing. He could see how her breasts were straining against the thin material of the dress. He said, "Well, Miss Parsons, or Marianne, if I may—the sad news is that I don't have much here to eat, and on top of that, the horse feed is going bad. This town hasn't served a good meal in some time."

Verlene gave him a fierce look. "If you're the law, you have no right to hold us here, causing us to undergo hardships, when comfort is just down the street. We haven't broken any laws."

Longarm reached around and scratched the back of his

neck. "Well, ladies," he said. "I'm not all that sure about that. You are consorting with known outlaws. And for all I know, you're planning on robbing a bank with them or holding up a stage or a railroad train."

Verlene made a disgusted sound. "You know better than that. Now, we have the right to be given humane treatment. We have the right to food, to comfortable living accommodations. Now, can you furnish us with those or not? If not, then we're going to march straight out that door and go down the street to where we can get them."

Longarm looked at her, frowning slightly. "Ladies, I don't want to have to put that other pair of handcuffs to work, but if you force me to, I will. I don't think you'll like very much being chained up, and I won't like doing it, so for the time being, you might as well shut up that kind of talk. But you do have a point that you have a right to food and shelter, and as a representative of the United States Government, it's my job to see that you get it. Let me put my mind to this thing for a moment. As it is, I was out of food myself. You sure you didn't bring none of that in the buggy?"

Marianne said, "Mrs. Minnie gave us to understand that the gentlemen we were coming to see would have ample provisions as well as a good assortment of beverages. She said we wouldn't want for anything."

Longarm made a sound like laughing, although he wasn't feeling humorous. "Maybe they do. It seems like a very unlikely place to be treated like you were staying at the Palmer House in Chicago. Let me set my mind to thinking on this subject and let me see what I can come up with."

Verlene said, "Well, I wish you would hurry up, Marshal. Some of us haven't had anything to eat since break-fast.''

"Yes, and some of us didn't even have breakfast," Longarm said.

"Nobody is forcing you to be out here. Why don't you get on your horse and go back to wherever it is that you came from?"

"Because I am here because of what's here and that's what I came for, understand? Now, be quiet."

Longarm thought a moment more, and then suddenly smiled. He said, "Hell, yes. Why not?"

Without another word, he got up from his chair and walked out into the stable. He reached into his pocket for the key to the handcuffs as he walked. Minnie saw him over her shoulder as he came near, and she began making agitated motions with her head. He said, "Just calm down, Minnie. I'm fixing to turn you loose. I've got a little job for you."

As quickly as he could, he took the handcuffs off her wrists and tucked them in his pocket. Then, before she could use her own hands, he untied the handkerchief. The moment her mouth was free, she started in cursing, swearing, yelling, and flailing her arms all about.

He grabbed her by the shoulders. He said in a flat hard voice, "Shut up, or I'll handcuff you again. Don't make another sound. Do you understand me?"

It took a few moments, but she finally settled down enough so that he could talk to her. He said, "I've got a chore for you. It's an easy one."

She gave him a suspicious look. "What kind of chore?"

"I want you to go to the big house at the end of the street where your boyfriend lives, J.J. Hunsacker. Tell him

60

that these girls are starving down here and that you need to get some food for all of you.''

She stared at him, startled by the request.

He said, ''Do you think you could do that?''

She continued to stare at him for another long moment. Finally, she said, ''Yes, I can do that. The question is: *Am* I going to do that? I'll tell you one thing, Mr. Marshal, and you had better get it straight off. I ain't leaving you alone with those two girls without a damned good reason.''

Longarm said, ''How about if they tell you to go up there? I reckon they're just about hungry enough to do it.''

She narrowed her eyes at him. He thought, looking at her, that she wasn't half as plain as she'd first appeared. She did have a little wear and tear, but some of it was becoming. She said, ''I ain't got nothing but the greatest case of dislike for you that there is, Mr. Marshal. If I do you any favors, it won't be for the sake of doing you any but for all of our sakes. You want me to go up there and ask Mr. Hunsacker for some grub? What makes you think I won't just stay with him up there?''

Longarm said, ''I am counting on you planning on staying close to your stock in trade. I don't reckon that you'd let those girls go without your vigilant eye any more than a butcher wouldn't watch his steaks. Am I right about that?''

Minnie Sewell said grimly, ''Just don't get any ideas about those girls. You haven't got the price in your pocket, Mr. Marshal, for either one of them.''

Longarm gave her a mocking laugh. He said, ''Oh, do you sell them as a pair?''

Mrs. Sewell straightened her clothes, which had become disarrayed in her struggle with the handcuffs. She said, ''I am going to go, but it's not for any good for you that will come from it. How am I supposed to know that Mr. Hunsacker will help us out on this?''

Longarm said, ''Oh, I think he will. After all, those two girls are his cattle that he'll be feeding. I think he will be more than happy to cooperate while he figures out a way to come down here and shoot me full of holes.''

Minnie Sewell looked at him with a hard eye. ''The sooner the better. That's what I say.''

''All right, the sooner the better that you go and get that food, and get enough for four while you are at it. I haven't been grazing too high on the hog lately myself.''

She turned away and started toward the office. ''I'll just tell the young ladies what I'm about.''

Longarm was right behind her. ''We'll tell them together so we'll both get the special thanks.''

She flashed him a hard look over her shoulder and said, ''I told you to get that kind of thinking out of your mind.''

It did not take the three women long to reach an agreement that they all needed some food, and without further argument with Longarm, Minnie Sewell was very shortly out the door and hurrying up the street as if she were escaping from prison. Longarm walked back into the office and looked at the two young women. He said, ''Well, Maw has gone to the store to fetch us some vittles. I ain't real sure, however, that she'll be coming back.''

Marianne said, ''Minnie Sewell is not the kind to run out on her friends. If she's going to Mr. Hunsacker's to fetch something to eat, you can be sure she'll be back.''

Verlene said, ''Yeah, and pretty quick too.''

Longarm put his feet up on the desk and yawned. ''We will see. I'm betting that we've seen the last of her. I'm betting that I'm going to have to take you two to Reno with me in order to draw them vultures out of that stone nest they've got built over there.''

Verlene and Marianne turned out to be right. Within two hours, Minnie Sewell was back with a tin pail filled with different kinds of foods. Longarm thought she looked a little mussed. It appear that the wind or somebody's hand had rearranged her hair, but he didn't say anything. He was too interested in what she was carrying in the pail to inquire into her personal affairs.

She had brought cheese, canned beans, canned tomatoes, canned peaches, some smoked beef, and some smoked ham. Longarm thought that, if nothing else, the Hunsackers were certainly eating a lot better than he and his little flock of prisoners. Minnie Sewell also brought something else: word from J.J. Hunsacker. She said, cocking her head, "J.J. said that if you don't turn me and those two girls loose right quick, he's going to find a way to separate you from your sanity.''

Longarm laughed lightly. "Well, Minnie, why don't you trot right on back up there and tell him that he is not going to separate me from my sanity until he comes out from that stone fort. Now, I'd like nothing more than a chance to see him try, him and his boys, but they are going to have to come outside to do it. I will not play inside. My momma told me not to be roughhousing inside the house.''

She gave him a look. "You think you're so damned smart, don't you?''

"Not so that you'd notice. If I was smart, first of all, I wouldn't be here. Second, I wouldn't be a deputy marshal, and third, I'd be in a lot nicer part of the country. So, what

I'm doing right now proves that I don't think I'm very smart.''

They found some pots and a skillet in Longarm's saddlebags. He built a fire, and the women heated some beans and tomatoes. Mrs. Sewell had brought along three tin plates, none for Longarm. He said, ''It doesn't matter—I've got my own. I thank you very much for choosing to omit me.''

As they ate what was a combination of breakfast and lunch, he watched the three women, deciding when and how much he was going to tell them. During Minnie Sewell's absence, he had reached a decision. The only way to get the Hunsackers out from that stone fort was to make them believe that something they wanted was shortly going to be out of reach. He was going to have to leave and take the women with him, and depend on J.J. and the rest of the boys to get their noses right down next to the ground and come a-yelping and running like a herd of hound dogs.

He didn't know exactly how he was going to do it. He didn't know if he could handle three females, all of them pulling in different directions. You couldn't just pull a gun on a woman—she knew you weren't going to shoot her. He didn't think he could manhandle all three of them at the same time. The question of how to get all three of them going in the right direction was an important one. He knew once he got them out in the desert, he wouldn't have any trouble. Nobody was going to jump out of the buggy in the big middle of nowhere without any water or food or any protection from the sun.

He put off thinking about it until he was finished eating. When he had mopped up his plate with a piece of bread, and had chewed it slowly and thoughtfully, he said, ''Minnie, I want you and Verlene and Marianne to go on back in the office and take yourselves a chair and sit right still.''

Mrs. Sewell was getting up to scrape the skillet out. She looked at him and said, ''What are you up to, Mr. Marshal?''

''It doesn't matter what I'm up to,'' Longarm said, shaking his head. ''Just do what I tell all three of you. When you get finished, all of you get in the office and stay there. Don't be looking out the window. Don't be looking out the door. Just stay in there and be quiet.''

Verlene said, ''Well, aren't we the high-handed one? I guess you think you can push us around any which way you choose.''

Longarm nodded. ''Just when it comes to government business. No more than that.'' He waited until they had gone into the office and closed the door behind them. He didn't want them seeing him making preparations for their departure.

He walked to the end of the livery stable, away from the street entrance, and pushed and shoved on the big door there and got it open far enough so that the buggy and the mule would pass through. After that, he untied the mule from the front part of the stable and took him to the back door and tied him there. He then saddled one of his horses and put the other on a halter lead. He tied both of them to the back of the buggy. Probably he was going to have to drive the buggy himself until he got a little ways away from the deserted town. He thought the women would be willing to ride along, figuring that sooner or later he would have to release them and they could return to Lodestar. They had another think coming. Until he got J.J. Hunsacker and his boys in hand, the women were his permanent bait.

With the buggy in place, he opened the door to the office and called for Minnie Sewell to come out. She got up reluctantly from her chair, grumbling, "Now, what do you want?"

"I want you to come along with me, Minnie, and take a look at something. It has to do with this buggy of yours." He closed the door to the office behind him, and then walked by her as they headed toward the buggy.

She said, "What the hell did you move back here for?"

He took her firmly by the left arm. "You've noticed that, have you?"

She tried to stop and jerk her arm loose from his. She said, "Let me go, you rascal. What's your plan here?"

With a grim face and a closed mouth, he manhandled her onto the buggy and on up into the backseat. Before she could move, he had handcuffed her wrist to one of the wrought-iron arms of the seat. She let out a squall, but it didn't matter—he had the madam in place now.

He walked back to the office just as Verlene was coming out, summoned by Minnie Sewell's squalls. She took in the scene with a quick glance and started to turn on Longarm. She was too late. He had anticipated her move, and already had her by the upper arms and was hustling her toward the buggy. For some reason, she made no outcry. She didn't go along docilely, but neither did she put up much of a fight. He propped her in the seat beside Minnie Sewell, and quickly handcuffed her right wrist to the arm of the backseat just as he had the older woman. He turned and went back after Marianne.

Longarm had left her for last because he had expected her to be the most docile of the three women, causing the least amount of trouble. But he was totally wrong. She

66

fought, from the first moment he had to pull her up to her feet, until he got her tied down in the front of the buggy. In the end, he had to gag her, fearing that her bloodcurdling cries would draw attention from the stone house even as far down the street as it was. She had scratched his face and his hands, but he could still remember feeling her firm young breasts as he was trying to subdue her. He had not sought the proud flesh barely concealed by the thin material of the dress and her underclothes, but it had seemed to find its way to the softest part of his hands.

Now, he stood beside the buggy, breathing heavily, mostly from the exertion of fighting the strong young woman, but also from the images and the feel of her body that had inflamed his brain.

Then he said, "Now, dammit, Marianne. You had better behave yourself from here on in. I am not going to stand for any more of that foolishness. I've got a job to do and if it comes to it, I'll bind you up like a market-bound hog and lay you on the floorboard."

For answer, she turned her head and gave him a murderous look with her eyes. His handkerchief, which had once gagged Minnie Sewell, was now across her lips.

He said, "All right. We're going to take a little ride. I want you all to sit steady. You ain't going nowhere as tied up as you are and handcuffed as you are, but I don't want you to scare that mule and get him to kicking the buggy to pieces. At the same time, that mule could break a bone amongst you three."

He looked around to make sure he had everything. His rifle was in the boot of the saddle. His derringer was in his pocket, and his spare revolver was in the saddlebags, along with his spare clothes and socks and what little money he had with him. There wasn't really anything else left to take. He had two full canteens of water, but that wasn't as important as it might have seemed since there would be no place to water the mules or the horses, and if they gave out in the desert, it wouldn't matter how much water you had in the canteen.

He took the time to walk to the front of the livery and offer a glance down at the big stone house at the end of the street. He saw no one, neither near the house nor anywhere near the street. After that, he walked back to the livery and looked out the rear. It was still clear. The horses were behind the buggy, the buggy was loaded, and his passengers were loaded. There was nothing left but to get up there himself and take the reins and start out.

As he untied the reins of the mule, he could not help but take note of the fact that they were going out in the middle part of the afternoon, into the heat of the day. It wouldn't take long for him or the women or the animals to wilt under the unrelenting sun. But he had chosen the time because he thought it most likely that Hunsacker and his sons would not be expecting him to be take off then for open spaces, not in that country, at that time of year. Most likely, they were having a nap themselves in the coolness of the big thick building.

The mule and the horses had had their chance at the water trough. He flipped the reins over the dashboard of the buggy, and then climbed up beside Marianne, who was bound hand and foot. With a deft move, he circled the mule around a stall post and headed him toward the big daylight gap in the back of the livery.

They went out into the heat and light at a faster pace than Longarm had meant to, but then the mule seemed to have a mind of his own. Longarm was willing to let him express it so long as he didn't work himself to death. He acted like a mule that was ready to head to the barn. Longarm had little doubt that he could loosen the reins on the animal and the mule would take them straight to wherever the mining camp was that the women had come from. Not that Longarm was going to do that, because a mule was a mule and he had the sense of a mule, and no mule was smart enough to know that he couldn't last at a running trot across the hot desert for ten miles. This mule was no exception. So with firm but steady pressure, Longarm pulled the animal back down into a trot and then a walk, and then slowed him down even more than that, heading him in the northwesterly direction that the mule had naturally taken as they'd left the livery stable.

Longarm forced himself not to look back until he had judged that they had traveled for half a mile. Then he glanced back toward the town of Lodestar. It looked very still, very deserted. There was no movement, no sign of anyone rushing to get on their trail. Longarm frowned slightly. He didn't want to get away clean. He wanted them coming after them. Dragging bait in front of a mountain lion wasn't much of a trick if the mountain lion wouldn't cooperate. He wasn't interested in seeing these women home. He was interested in luring J.J. Hunsacker and his gang out into open where one man would have a chance against the six or seven of them or however many there were.

But Longarm was not too worried about having gotten away cleanly. He had a pretty good idea that he had been watched at frequent intervals ever since the women had arrived. He had not necessarily seen anyone, but he had felt their presence from a distance. He didn't expect that J.J. Hunsacker was fool enough to let his prize sit so close and not keep an eye on it. Longarm had never yet ascertained which girl went with which Hunsacker, including Mrs. Sewell. Not that it made much difference.

For now, he settled down to the serious business of driving a mule across the desert. The women seemed to be riding all right. The buggy top provided some relief from the sun, though nothing could provide relief from the unrelenting dead air and heat that surrounded them and seemed to almost suffocate them. He wasn't afraid of the Hunsackers attacking him with rifles at long range. They weren't about to do that out of fear of hitting the women. He had protection as good as a man was likely to get.

After a while, he snapped the reins on the mule's back and let him speed his walk up, but now the mule wasn't as responsive, and Longarm could tell that the heat was already going to work on at least one animal. He glanced back and saw that Verlene and Minnie Sewell were riding along stoically, looking to be none the better for the afternoon outing.

Now that they were clear, he saw no reason to keep the gag on Marianne. With his right hand, he reached over, and with his strong fingers, undid the knot and pulled it away. He expected a barrage of cussing, but all she did was pant. The heat was getting to her too. He took the reins in his teeth, and reached over and untied her hands where they lay in her lap. She gave him a half-grateful look of appreciation when the knots fell free from her flesh. She rubbed the reddened skin with each hand alternately.

They rode on across the desolate desert. The mule was quite content now to stay in a medium walk. Longarm was surprised that he had not had more protest from his backseat passengers, but he'd congratulated himself too soon. Verlene's voice came suddenly to his ears. She said, "Listen, Marshal. Where the hell do you think that you are taking us? You could get us killed out here in this desert."

Longarm said, "I'm taking you to safety, if that be its name. I'm taking you away from danger—danger posed by the Hunsacker gang, who are outlaws. If you become joined up with them, that would make you an outlaw too and I'd have to put you in jail."

From the front seat, Marianne said, "Oh, don't try that old story on us. We know very well what you are doing."

Longarm watched the mule's ears to see if they'd heard anything that his inferior pair hadn't. He said, "What am I supposed to be up to?"

Marianne said, "You're taking us off for your own self. We understand men like you, but you won't get away with it."

Minnie Sewell said in a sullen voice, "I've got some news for you, mister. You get us out in the open out here, and J.J. Hunsacker is going to fill you full of holes. You're going to look like an old dress that somebody left whipping in the wind."

Longarm looked around into the rear seat of the buggy. He said thoughtfully, "You know, Minnie, you're saying that just to get at me, but you might turn out to be right. I am taking a hell of a chance here and there ain't no maybes about it."

She stared back at him, too startled by his agreement to comment any further.

Chapter 5

It seemed that with every moment the heat increased, until Longarm didn't see how it could get much hotter without everything bursting into flames. They plodded along on his northwesterly course. The only thing that disturbed the flat, featureless landscape was a big outcropping of rock amid what appeared to be trees. The outcropping lay just to the right of his line of march, and was, he guessed, about three or four miles distant. In that heat, and in that country, that was a pretty good ways.

The women had lapsed into silence, content only to spend their energy in a futile attempt to fan a breeze into their face with their hands. Longarm was soaked with sweat. The mule was holding up fairly well, but Longarm was considering hitching one of the horses to the side of the harness and seeing if the horse couldn't take some strain off the mule and help him along a little.

From time to time, Longarm looked back at the deserted town of Lodestar. He guessed they had come some four or five miles in the hour they had been traveling. The place remained quiet. The buildings had shrunk in the distance, but they were still as solitary and as silent and as lonely. He glanced out ahead at the outcropping, wondering about it. He was used to seeing rock buttes in the desert, but these looked big. The heat waves shimmered off the desert floor and distorted shapes and distances so that a man had no real idea of what he was looking at or how far off it was.

The desert had taken an upturn, and the mule had slowed as he dragged the buggy up the slight incline of sand, cactus, and rock. For the tenth time, Longarm asked the women if he was on the right course for the mining camp. None of them bothered to even open their mouth on this occasion. Before, they had favored him with some choice cuss words, which had sounded strange coming out of such angelic-looking mouths—at least two of them had angelic-looking mouths. But they seemed under no compulsion to give him the slightest hint or direction. He hadn't worried. He figured the heat and the sun and the discomfort would do his work for him, causing the women to suddenly get cooperative, if for no other reason than for their own sake.

The mule had nearly reached the top of a rise. Longarm could tell that the long pull up the elevation in the desert had taken a lot out of the mule. He was determined to rest the animal at the top. As they pulled up, he stopped the mule right on the small crest. Now that he was looking downhill, the outcropping of big rocks looked much different. Looking back, he could see that the town of Lodestar was indeed in a valley, if you could say that a desert had valleys.

The mule was standing with his head down, and Longarm could see his ribs heaving in and out as he breathed.

It was clear that they were going to lose the mule if Longarm didn't give the creature some help. He got out of the buggy, taking both canteens with him, and went up to the head of the harness, where the mule was standing quite still. Longarm took off his hat, poured one of the canteens into the crown, and then offered it to the mule. The animal accepted the water and drank greedily, spilling as much as he was drinking. Longarm finished pouring the canteen into his hat, and let the mule keep on drinking. There had been a full five gallons when they had started, but he reckoned now there were only three gallons, and the mule could handle that much and more. Longarm opened the second canteen and gave the mule more water. It was playing hell with his hat, but he needed another one anyway. Besides, it was very doubtful that he needed to cut much of a figure of fashion where they were headed.

When he was through with the mule, he put his hat back on. It felt wonderfully cool under the blazing sun. He walked back to the buggy with one empty canteen and the other only half full. It was a serious matter to have as little water as they did and to be where they were now. He was going to remark on it to the women when he happened to glance toward the south, toward the deserted town. To his surprise, he saw several little black specks swirling around what he took to be the livery stable. He also saw several in front of the stone house at the end of the street. It was apparent that the Hunsackers had come alive and realized that they, he and the women, had left. Longarm supposed the Hunsackers could see him and the women just as well.

He looked around, not quite certain what to do next. Apparently, he was going to get his wish. He thought they would be having company is less time than it had taken them to travel this far. He expected that the Hunsackers were riding desert-hardened horses and that they would be bringing plenty of water. He needed to get to cover. He glanced over his left shoulder. The rocky outcropping had not moved. It appeared to be no more than a couple of miles away. It was best, he thought, to get started. That is, unless the women wanted to tell him where the diggings were and if they were even close.

He climbed into the buggy and took up the reins. The mule seemed more alert and lively now that he had had some water, and stepped off as they started downhill. Longarm resisted the urge to lift him into a trot. Whatever energy the mule had, he was going to need when they were on the flat.

From the backseat, Minnie Sewell said, ''I see that they are coming.''

Longarm turned his head and looked back at her. ''That's right, Minnie. At least they're outside. I don't know if they have figured out where we are or not, but you can bet if they can find a bed in the dark, they can pick up our trail leaving that town. Now, I know it's your hope that they are going to shoot me to pieces, but I want to remind you all of something. I don't plan to let them get close enough to just concentrate on me. So go to thinking about bullets whizzing around your ear and trimming your hair for you. See what you think of that.''

Marianne said, ''They wouldn't shoot at us.''

Longarm said, ''I didn't say they would, but I'm going to stick mighty close to you three, and if they are going to shoot at me, they're going to be shooting mighty close to you.''

From the backseat, Verlene's voice snapped out, ''That's

76

a coward. There's nothing of a gentleman about that.''

Longarm laughed wearily. "Verlene, I wish the bunch of you would get it straight in your mind that I'm a United States deputy marshal. I ain't a gentleman and I'm not brave, at least not any braver than I have to be. I don't see any point in being brave when it's six or seven against one. Now, do any of you want to tell me where that miners camp is? Are we anywhere close to it?''

Minnie Sewell said, "You'll not get anything from us, Mr. Smart Aleck.''

Longarm nodded. "All right. Have it the way you will.''

He put the reins under his knee and held them back with pressure against the seat while he picked up his lever-action carbine off the floor. He worked the lever and put a shell into the chamber. Then he reached into his pocket, took another .44-caliber cartridge, and shoved it into the magazine of the rifle so that it now held seven shells. He glanced over at Marianne. "You be sure and point out the one that is intended to be your fiancé and I'll shoot him clean.''

She gave him a sour look and said, "You're not making yourself real welcome with us.''

Longarm spat over the side. "Lady, I ain't trying try make myself at home with you. You'd better make yourselves at home with *me* because you are going to be with me a hell of a lot longer than you think.''

Minnie Sewell said, "I think they're going to be wrapping you up in your best shirt, if you take my meaning.''

Longarm chuckled. "Oh, I take your meaning, Minnie. I just think I'm going to thin that bunch out a good deal before that happens.''

He looked back over his shoulder, but the rise that he'd topped blocked his view. He could not know if the Hunsackers were pursuing him or not, but for the next half hour, he began to get edgy. The mule was showing signs of fatigue, and Longarm was wondering if the fortress of the rocks was actually coming any nearer. He had visions of being trapped out in the desert flat with nothing more for protection than a buggy and three women. It was not an inviting prospect. He had no doubt about his ability to hold the Hunsackers at bay with a little cover, but he wasn't swimming in ammunition. There were forty or fifty cartridges in his saddlebags—a half a box—and in a running gunfight, that many caps could be busted in no time at all.

After another hour, Longarm could tell that the mule was definitely flagging, slowing down more and more. Longarm was going to have to do something and do it fast. He pulled the mule to a stop and jumped down from the buggy, taking his rifle as he did. He went to the back, untied the horse that was already saddled, and stepped aboard, shoving the rifle into the boot. Then he reined his horse around the buggy and up to the head, where the mule was panting a little harder than it should have been.

Longarm ordinarily didn't carry a rope with him, but he had one on this occasion. He threw a noose in it and used it to take a grip a on the twin shafts, intending to give the mule a little help. He dallied the rope off around the horn of his saddle, and then set out to take up some of the strain off the mule. As they started forward and the buggy jolted into motion, he was surprised to see Marianne slide over in the seat and take up the reins. Longarm noted with more surprise that she had just enough pull on the reins to give the mule something to lean against as they worked their way across the desert floor.

As he was mounted on horseback, Longarm had a much

clearer view behind him. Not only that, but as they had drifted to the right, the rise had flattened and he could see parts of the deserted mining town of Lodestar and the black dots that had been scurrying around it. Now, the dots had formed into one pack and were moving in a definite direction, toward him. It was a guess, but he judged that they were some five or six miles away, perhaps further, but they were on good horses and he knew it wouldn't take them long to catch up. He had very little time to spare.

Urging his horse, Longarm hurried the mule along as best he could. The rock outcropping didn't seem to be coming any nearer, but he knew it was. The desert played tricks on your eyes. Things could look awfully far off and yet be reasonably close by, and by the same token, something you thought was only a mile off, you'd spend the better part of the day killing your horse to get to.

The two women in back were leaning around as much as their handcuffs would allow them to look out the back of the buggy to see where the Hunsackers were. Marianne was holding the reins and helping the mule along. Or at least that was the way it appeared to Longarm, but he wasn't quite convinced. If he hadn't had a rope on the shaft of the buggy, he wouldn't have put it past the young woman to suddenly jerk the mule around and try to beat it back toward the Hunsackers. The mule wouldn't have made it, of course, but there would have been no end of trouble. He wanted that mule to survive until it got to the shadow and help of the rocks. If he knew anything about deserts, there was a good chance the place, which was growing bigger and bigger with every step they took in its direction, would be full of cool, dark caves. Their most immediate concern was water. Two gallons of water wasn't going to split very well between one mule, two horses, and four people.

He hurried the whole contraption along, figuring he could get into the rocks before the Hunsacker party could draw near. Longarm guessed them to be no more than two and a half miles off, and he still had a half mile to the rocks. They were coming fast, but he wondered how much horse they would have left by the time they made that last drive. He also knew that if they got within a quarter of a mile, he could slow them down considerably with his rifle. He hated to shoot horses, but he knew the quickest way to kill a man in the desert was to shoot his horse down. Horses couldn't carry double in these kind of conditions.

He glanced again at the rocks, and then back at the Hunsackers. They were still just a shapeless mob, no figures visible, but he figured the old man would be in the very forefront. It almost made him smile to himself, but he reckoned J.J. Hunsacker was curious about the whole state of affairs, and he knew that sending Minnie Sewell down for some grub for the girls and himself must have irritated Hunsacker no little bit. But the old man hadn't had a choice. He could not feed the women without feeding Longarm.

Longarm glanced toward the inside of the buggy, and was startled to see that Marianne had slipped quietly over to the side and dropped to the sand. As fast as he could, he untied the rope from his saddlehorn, dropped it, then wheeled his horse around and caught up with the girl before she had taken a half-dozen steps back toward the pursuing outlaws.

Longarm leaned down out of the saddle, grabbed her around the waist with his left arm, and lifted her up in front of him. She was light, and felt almost like a feather, except that she was squirming and kicking like a wildcat. She yelled in his face, "Let me go, you sonofabitch! Let me go! Take your big hands off of me!"

He turned his horse back toward the buggy and caught up with it. The mule was still walking patiently ahead, although his pace had slowed since Marianne had dropped the reins. Longarm rode up to his head, stopped the animal, and carried a protesting Marianne back to the buggy and shoved her inside. With her fighting him all the while, he retied her hands and her feet. He said, "Now, there. See if you can jump out of the buggy now. If you keep on yelling, I'm going to gag you. Do you want me to stick this back in your mouth?"

He pulled the bandanna out of his pocket and showed it to her. "Do you care for some more of this?"

She gave him a spiteful look. "Oh, you just go to hell, Mr. Big Man. You just think you're so tough. Well, you just wait until yet get caught and those gentlemen behind you make you holler."

Longarm smiled. "Well, to begin with, there ain't no gentlemen behind us. If you're talking about that bunch of outlaws and renegades and bushwhackers, that's the Hunsackers. You really don't want any part of them, but you don't know that yet. They'll put twenty years on your life overnight.

"But I don't plan on them to catch up with us. See, they're doing what I wanted them to do, which was come out into the open. That was the only way I was going to be able to trap them and then catch them. I know that puts a sour look on your face, but it's the truth of the matter. I did want them to come out. They're chasing me just so I can catch them."

From the backseat, Minnie Sewell said, "Oh, pshaw. That's just so much big talk. You know as well as I do if they catch you, you're just one dead sonofagun. Them Hunsackers will teach you and your grandmother to suck eggs."

Longarm stepped away from the buggy, went to his horse, led him around to the other side of the mule, and picked up the rope.

He said, "We're going to move a little swifter now, so you all just take it easy."

Minnie Sewell said, "Can't you at least unhandcuff us? Keeping us in chains like this is downright unhuman. What would happen if this mule were to run away? We could all be killed, the way you've got us manacled in irons here to the buggy seats."

Longarm smiled as he stepped aboard his horse and took a dally around his saddlehorn with the rope that was tied to the buggy. He said, "Don't worry, Minnie. If this mule were to run away, it would be a miracle about like it raining this afternoon. It's all this mule can do to keep on walking. I may have to bring that other horse on up here to help him."

Longarm quickened the pace slightly, though there was little danger of the Hunsackers coming up on them before they could be safely into the rocks. His biggest concern was what he was going to find when they finally did get in amongst the outcropping. He assumed that there would be a place where they could fort up, where they would have protection on all four sides, but that might turn out to be wishful thinking. For all he knew, what he was looking at could be just a line of rocks running east and west across the desert floor with no way to protect your back, no matter which side of the rocks you were on.

But then the rocks were so close, he could see the work of the wind and the weather. The outcropping was fairly tall, some forty to fifty feet in height for the majority of the butte-like humps. One big butte in the center went up like a giant chimney, rising perhaps a hundred feet. It was accompanied on each side by humps no less jagged and no less craggy.

As they neared, he was able to see a sight he was looking for—the outcropping was circular. He was able to tell that as he turned and led his party to the west or the left side of the group of rocks. Then an opening appeared, and he turned his horse, followed by the mule and the buggy, into the center of the rock formation.

It was almost like a little room without a roof. It was not so little, being perhaps fifty to sixty yards in one direction and twenty to thirty in the other, but it was good protection. No one could slip up on him and take him unawares without giving themselves away. As near as he could tell, there were only two openings in the wall of rock. One to the north and the smaller one to the west. He had no intention of letting the Hunsackers ever learn that there was a northerly approach. He was going to keep them bottled up to the south.

He led his party to the edge of the rock toward the lower portion of the outcropping. To his surprise and delight, he could see the mouths of several caves set in the earth between some of the big boulders. Some of them were six and seven feet high, a good place to hide the women and the horses and keep them out of the way of flying lead.

He made his way through the scattered rock lying on the

ground to the main wall of stone that had thrust up through the soil. He found a cleft in the rocks, and he was able to see the Hunsacker party in pursuit. He watched them as they came on over the rising and falling desert floor.

They weren't coming particularly fast. He reckoned they were finding out in a hurry that it was best, in such country, not to just jump on the nearest horse and set out in hot pursuit. He reckoned they were already wishing they had taken some time to better organize themselves, and maybe take along an extra horse or two, before they went running around in the Nevada desert. But Longarm figured that the minute they had realized that he had absconded with the ladies, the alarm had gone off and they had jumped up and got high behind.

He reckoned they were still at least a mile and a half away. At the rate they were going, he figured he had an hour, and that was plenty of time. He stepped down from the rock he was standing on and walked down the wall of stone. He came to the first cave mouth and stepped inside. He was disappointed to see that it was only a few feet deep and would serve for nothing unless a body just wanted to get out of the sun.

But the next mouth, which was at least six feet high, led back and downward. He walked ten feet into the cave, and after hearing the squeaking of a few bats that he had disturbed, he figured it would be perfect. It might be a block long. It might be no more than twenty feet long. He couldn't see, as dark as it was, but it would serve. He walked back out into the sunshine and started toward the buggy. He could see the women sitting stiffly where they were.

He came up to the buggy without a face being turned

84

toward him. It almost made him want to smile. But these were three ladies who were not going to affect him with either their charms or their lack thereof. He leaned his rifle against one wheel of the buggy, then untied Marianne, and then released the other two from their handcuffs, stuffing the manacles into his back pocket, putting the key in his right pocket.

As the women stepped down stiffly from the buggy, he said, "Take a good look at your new home and get used to it. Now, if you want to run out there into that desert and try to meet the boyfriends and the old man, you are welcome to do it. There's going to be lead flying here in about a half hour, and I would say that the chances are that you are going to be hit. And if you don't get hit, you're probably going to die of thirst out here, because you're not going to get to your fiancés. I'm going to be keeping them busy with my own rifle fire. Now, I've got a place for you to stay and I want you to get out ahead of me. I'll show you where it is."

He tried to herd them toward the cave he had in mind, but a smaller one off to his left had taken his eye, and he thought it would be worthwhile to investigate. He pointed out to Minnie Sewell where they could get shelter from the sun, and then set out on his own toward the smaller-mouthed cave. He was carrying his carbine in his right hand.

He said, as he parted from the women, "If you try to run, I may take it into my head to shoot one of you in the ankle. And I damned sure wouldn't go near that mule or those horses. In the first place, that mule is probably going to die if you take him more than a quarter of a mile, and

85

those horses belong to me and that would make you a horse thief.''

He watched as they made their way over the rock-strewn desert floor heading toward the shade of the second cave. He turned and made his way to the third cave he had seen. It was mostly hidden by a big rock that had fallen from above. It turned out to have a fairly big mouth. The angle he had seen it from, with the rock in the way, had caused it to look much smaller. He walked up to the rock and, leaning his head down slightly, entered the cave.

The first sound and the first smell he got made his ears and mouth prick up. With a few steps, the sunlight still lighting that part of the cave, he saw a small but steady stream bubbling out of the ground and then running down-hill away from the mouth. It was an underground spring, and it couldn't have been better located. By the sign of campfires and tallow from candles, he could tell the place had been used before—either by Indians or outlaws, he didn't know which—but he did know that he now had water for the horses. He did know too that he had better hurry. He wanted to get them watered and put up before the Hunsackers arrived.

He hurried out of the cave and across the open ground to where the mule and the buggy and his horses were. As quickly as he could, he unharnessed the mule, and then untied his horse from the back. Then, leading all three animals, he took them around the rocks and into the cave. They had all smelled the water, and they were all anxious and in a hurry to get to the source.

Longarm had to keep a tight hold on them, but he was able to take all the animals into the cave at once and let them drink from the underground spring. He himself wanted a drink badly, but he knew he could wait until the horses and the mule were through. He let them drink for ten or fifteen minutes, just long enough to satisfy them for the time being, but not enough to cause them to founder or to bloat. When they had had enough, he pulled and tugged them reluctantly away from the spring, and then led them along a ledge to the cave where the women had gone. When he led the horses in, the women set up a squawk. Minnie Sewell said, "We don't want them damned animals in here! Get them out of there! We've already got bats!"

Longarm said, "These horses need shade as bad as you do, so just shut up, Minnie. Keep these horses up on this end. I don't know what's back there. It could be a drop-off, it could be a black hole back there that you could fall into and never stop falling until you hit China. So keep these horses and this mule up here toward the mouth of this cave. You don't know, you might need them in case the Hunsackers put a bullet in me."

Verlene said, "You're going to let us go, that's what is going to happen."

Longarm said, "Lady, was I you, I'd stay in this cave and keep my mouth shut. If you want to run to your boy-friend, now's the time. There's a chance that you might make it before you die."

Marianne said, "You think you're so smart. You just make me sick, Marshal. Did you know that?"

Longarm chuckled. "I'm liable to make you more than that before this is all over with, Marianne, but you go ahead and think what you want to."

He started out of the cave, and then turned back to say, "By the way, there's another cave about ten yards to the right that's got a running spring in it, in case you're thirsty.

One of you might want to go to the buggy and get that basket of grub that Mrs. Sewell so kindly got for us from J.J. Hunsacker. Might be that you're going to get a little hungry, staying here in this cave.''

Minnie Sewell said, ''Are you telling the truth when you say that if we want to make a run for it, now is the time? You'd let us go? You wouldn't stop us? You wouldn't shoot us?''

Longarm looked at Minnie Sewell as if he wasn't hearing right. He said, ''If you're stupid enough to run out into that desert with a long two miles between you and any kind of help, you just do that. I don't think you'd last two hours, not unless you spend a considerable amount of time taking on water like a camel. But no, I don't care if you make a break for it, as you call it. Now, I've got to get to looking as to how I'm going to defend this place against your fiancés, who are apparently going to come riding up here with bad intent on their mind. But I've got some news for them. And remember this, Minnie, just in case you do try to get at them. I don't plan to let them get much closer than a half a mile, and that's a hell of a long ways to run across the desert floor.''

She looked at him, glaring with her hands on her hips. She said, ''I just may take you up on that, Marshal.''

He shrugged and left the cave, winding his way between the scattered rocks over to the buggy. He reached into the back and retrieved the saddlebags from the floor where he had left them. There wasn't much in them, just his extra revolver and the last of his ammunition, a clean shirt, a clean pair of jeans, and a clean pair of socks. He didn't figure to need the clothes, but he was going to need the ammunition, and he didn't figure it was going to be enough.

Standing by the buggy, he gave a careful look to the rock wall, searching for the most likely place to take up a defense. Finally, he settled on a spot where the rocks were all jumbled and it would be difficult for the Hunsackers to see where the fire was coming from, but where it still appeared to give a 180-degree view toward the south. Holding his rifle, with his saddlebags over his shoulder, he picked his way over to the spot. It was necessary to clamber up on several smaller rocks so that he was standing about five feet in the air.

He found that with the protruberance of the bigger rocks, there was a notch in the wall that gave him an excellent field of fire while affording him the most protection from incoming shots. Not that he was worried too much about their ability to fire back. They were going to be on the bald, bald desert, and they would have to stay out of range, and if they were out of range of his rifle, he was also out of range of theirs.

He climbed up into position, and then worked his shoulders until he was set in the notch of the rock wall. One glance told Longarm that the Hunsackers were not far off. By now, they were close enough that they had evolved into individual riders and he could take a count. He had expected six or seven, and he was amazed to find that nine men were coming toward him. Either they had gotten reinforcements, or there had been men in the house awaiting them.

He narrowed his eyes, squinting them to better see into the glazing sun and through the rising heat waves. He could easily pick out the old man, who was riding back in the back. His billowing, thick graying hair was easy to spot.

Up front, Longarm could see LeeRoy leading the pack.

To his right was the second oldest son, Shank. Longarm had never had any dealings with the young man, who he understood to be in his early to mid-twenties, but he had been told that Shank was the meanest of the lot. He had murdered and he had done robbed. Of course, that was no different from any of the rest of the Hunsackers, but it was said that Shank was known to relish his crimes.

Longarm didn't recognize any of the other men, though one of them appeared to be a man named Jim Stock who was a cousin to the Hunsackers. Longarm had come across him once before in a running gunfight as he and several sheriff's deputies had chased the gang into northern Arizona. If it was Jim Stock, it was a new problem, because Stock was said to be an excellent marksman, and it was said that he carried a rifle of greater firing distance than the average Winchester carbine, which was only accurate up to about a quarter of a mile. It was said that Stock carried a Sharps buffalo gun. If he did and it was sighted in, that made him dangerous from three times as far as the Winchester carbine.

Longarm watched the men coming on toward him, and thoughtfully put his thumb on the hammer of his rifle and drew it back, taking satisfaction from the *clitch-clatch* sound it made. The Hunsacker party was still a little too far away for a shot, but they were getting to the place where it would be time to thin their bunch out as much as he could and as fast as he could.

Then something flickered in the corner of his eye—some movement, some animation. He turned his head swiftly just in time to see Minnie Sewell vanish through the western entrance of the rock fort. He started to yell, but held his tongue for fear of giving away his position. He could not imagine what the woman was doing rushing out into the desert. He supposed that the woman thought she could make it to the Hunsacker party and that they would give her protection, but he had news for her. She was going to discover just how hard it was in the desert sand with the sun beating down on you so hard that it was driving you several inches deeper into the loose sand.

He waited, looking out the front of the little palisade of boulders with his eyes cut around to the right, waiting for Minnie to come hurrying around from where she had exited and appear heading toward the Hunsackers. It took a few moments, but he wasn't disappointed. Out into the sunlight, she staggered from the south side of the rocks. She was already struggling in the sand and sun, and she had only come some fifty yards. He would have yelled at her to get back to the safety of the rock outcrops, but he knew she wouldn't listen.

He watched as Minnie kept struggling across the sand, now and again falling to her hands and knees, and then rising quickly and going on. He noted that she had taken the canteen out of the buggy. He wondered if she had taken the time to fill it in the spring that was in the cave. He didn't really care, because she had clearly declared which side she was on. She was as much an opponent of the law as the Hunsackers.

Longarm brought his attention back to the advancing party. They were, he guessed, not too far out of range, and closing rapidly, or as rapidly as a horse could slowly walk. Now he could see how done in the mounts were. They were clearly dead tired, and most of them were covered with the white salty remains of dried sweat. He reckoned they didn't have much life left in them.

He sighted down the barrel of his rifle at Jim Stock, if indeed it was the man. But if it was, he posed the biggest threat, and Longarm had every intention of disposing of him as soon as possible. He was at the point of risking a long shot when a noise to his left made him raise his cheek from the rifle and glance quickly around.

There stood Marianne, looking, in spite of the dirt and dust and sweat and fatigue, as pretty as most girls could aspire to, even though she had a grim expression on her face. She said, "You had no right to let her go. You know how dangerous it is out there in that desert."

Longarm opened his mouth and stared at her. He said, "Are you crazy, girl? What in the hell are you talking about? I didn't let her go."

Marianne's eyes bored into him. Her bosom rose and fell, distracting his mind as he could see the nipples hard through the thin material of her dress. She said, "You could have stopped her. You would have stopped her if she had been one of us."

Longarm said, "If you'll recollect, I told you at the buggy that you were free to do what you wanted to do but that I wouldn't recommend you go racing off across the desert. You do remember me saying that?"

She shook her head angrily, making her hair swirl about her face. "Yes, but we're just women. You know what the desert is like, we don't. And now, Minnie has gone out there and anything could happen to her. You should have stopped her."

Longarm turned his face back to his rifle where he had it propped up between two small rocks. He said, "Well, I didn't. In the first place, I didn't see her until she was already outside. If you want to take a look at her, you can find a low place in these rocks and you will see that she is floundering along doing the best she can. It may not be good enough, but at least she is trying. If you look, I'd be damned careful because there's a man out there that's got the kind of a rifle that can reach from them to us, and he is going to shoot at any movement.''

She said, ''Oh, the hell with you.'' But there was not much conviction in her voice. She suddenly turned on her heels and walked back, heading toward the cave,where he supposed Verlene was with the horses and the mule. He watched her walk, admiring the sway of her hips and the dainty motion of her feet. He wondered what she would be like in bed, but he doubted that he was ever going to find out. As a general rule, working girls like her weren't much good when it was just for fun.

When he looked back, the Hunsackers were clearly within range. He moved his rifle sights around ever so gently so that he was focused on the broad chest of Jim Stock. Now he could see the man clearly. He was wearing the brocade vest that he was known to wear. His rifle was still in the boot, but Longarm had no doubt that this was a man who would cause him trouble. He leaned down over his sights, calculating the wind, calculating the distance, calculating the drop of the bullet. Then, very gently, he pulled the trigger, and the sharp crack of the shot rang harshly off the rocks.

Chapter 6

For an instant, it was if nothing had happened. Then Longarm saw Jim Stock duck his head as the bullet whistled
past him, and then he saw the party of men split in two,
the left going to the left of the shot and the right riding off
in *that* direction. Furious at missing, even though he knew
he had fired at too great a distance, Longarm quickly levered another shell into the chamber and sighted in on a man
riding behind and to the left of Stock.

This time, he held his sight on the man a little longer,
not allowing the shimmering heat waves to cause him to
aim too high. It was not a particularly hard shot because
the men were only walking their horses slowly. He
squeezed the trigger gently, felt the thump of the stock
against his shoulder, and then almost through the echo of
the explosion bounding off the encircling rocks, the man
that he had hit went backwards and sideways out of his
saddle. His horse stopped immediately as if someone had

jerked back on the reins. The man lay on the sand of the desert floor, not moving.

The man nearest him dismounted and came over and knelt down next to the body. It was clear that the prone rider wasn't going further. The rider that had dismounted caught up the dead man's horse, and then remounted, and they all started onward again, only now they were scattering to the left and the right, making Longarm's shots harder.

He wanted a shot at Shank. He figured that maybe Shank was the most dangerous of the bunch outside of Stock, but he could never quite get the man fully in his sights with the lines of sight offered him by his firing position. Instead, he settled on one of the other Hunsacker boys, one that looked like Joe. He fired, and saw the man clutch his thigh, and then suddenly jump down from his horse as it started to fall. The bullet had apparently just creased the man's flesh and then gone on into the horse. The horse was almost to the ground by the time the man was able to land on his feet and limp on around behind the animal before throwing himself to the sand, taking cover behind the dying animal.

Longarm cursed. He hated shooting horses. He levered in another shell and tried another shot at Joe, if that was who he had wounded. The bullet kicked up sand harmlessly a foot to the left.

But now J.J. Hunsacker was directing his men to fall back. He knew as well as Longarm did the range of Longarm's rifle, and he was directing his people to move a hundred yards to the rear. That was all right with Longarm. They could sit out there in the desert and fry for all he cared.

Suddenly, he became aware of Minnie Sewell, still struggling toward the party. She had made only some two hundred yards away from the rock face, and he wondered if she would make another two hundred, for by now she was staggering and floundering badly. He wondered if the old man would make a try to retrieve her. If he did, Longarm determined he would let him get away with it. Any man who was fool enough to ride into the covering fire just to save an old battle-ax deserved anything she could give him.

No horseman rode to Minnie's rescue. The old man didn't even seem to notice her as he wheeled his own horse around while shouting and gesturing for his men to get out of Longarm's rifle range. Longarm snapped off a shot at one trailing member of the gang, and was satisfied to see him pitch out of the saddle. It had been a long shot with long odds against him, but he had gotten lucky, at least this time. However, the shot had not done for the man. He had landed on his stomach, and almost immediately got to his feet, reached over for his horse's reins, and hurriedly limped toward the rear where Mr. Hunsacker was headed.

They had fired a few shots back, but they had done so out of frustration, knowing they were firing into a rock wall. The slugs had glanced and whined harmlessly away. Longarm doubted that any of the riflemen knew where he was holed up in his firing position.

His interest was once more drawn to Minnie Sewell. She had somehow gathered her strength, and was now marching resolutely across the hot sand. She had managed, however, to lose her canteen somewhere along the line. Longarm reckoned it had gotten too heavy for her. She was now out of range of his own rifle shot, so Hunsacker could easily send someone to fetch her into their midst.

They had all rounded up and dismounted some six hundred yards away from his position. They were standing around staring his way. He wondered just how they were going to like it when they realized that they didn't have any water. They didn't look like they had brought along any provisions either. He also wondered if they knew that he had water.

With a sudden stab of irritation, he realized he had let Minnie Sewell get away. She knew that he had a spring of water just inside his fort. That was a bad break. Now, they would attack him in a different fashion, knowing that he could hold out much longer than they would have previously expected. He had rather hoped for a long drawn-out battle of attrition during which he could take them down one by one, until there was some semblance of evenness between them and himself. Then he would have gone on the offensive and run them in the ground. Now he thought they would become bolder in their attack.

Of course, that depended on how bad the two oldest boys wanted Verlene and Marianne. They would be the ones pressing on the attack.

Longarm noticed that J.J. had spotted Minnie Sewell. He gestured to one of his men. It appeared to Longarm to be Joe, the next-oldest boy. Joe jumped on his horse, took the reins of another, and then carefully walked both animals across the desert until he came up to Minnie. He dismounted and helped her up into the saddle, her skirts billowing up around her waist, then remounted himself before they made their way to where J.J. Hunsacker and the others were waiting.

Longarm became aware of Marianne and Verlene standing beside him. They were peering out between the same gap where his rifle rested. They could see the scene as clearly as he could. He said, ''Well, looks like she made it.'' He shrugged. ''You could have gone with her.''

Marianne said, ''You'd no more let us go than you would jump from here to Reno.''

Longarm got an amused look on his face. He said, ''Well, Marianne. Whatever makes you think that?''

The blond-haired girl said, ''Because you think of us as bait. You don't fool me, Deputy Marshal Long. You're trolling them along with Verlene and me, ain't you?''

''Yeah, that could be,'' Longarm said.

''So, you'd no more let us get away then you'd fly. You'd have shot us if we'd try to make it, wouldn't you?''

Longarm shrugged. ''I ain't shot many women this year. I don't know how I'd have felt about it.''

''You didn't shoot Minnie because you didn't think she was worth it.''

''You have a point there, Marianne. I have to admit it. Now, I hope that you're wearing some perfume and the wind is blowing in the right direction, because I'd like to see it fetch Joe and LeeRoy in here on the run.''

Marianne stamped her foot. She said, ''You are a horrible man.''

Longarm nodded his head and spat on the floor of the rocks beneath his feet. He said, ''Yeah, that may be so, but I'm the only one wearing a badge.''

Marianne shook her head, making her golden hair fly. She said, ''You may not be as smart as you think you are. You think you are trying to trap Mr. Hunsacker and his boys, but it looks to me like you're the one who's trapped.''

Longarm gave her a small smile. ''Well, we'll see. Now, you two had better get back in that cave and get out of this sun. It'll fry your brains.''

"Well, then, I reckon that's something you don't have to worry about."

When they were gone, he got out his watch. It was just after five o'clock, but the sun was still high in the sky. He reckoned there would be no sunset for another three hours, and the heat would burn just as intensely during that time as it was at the moment.

He settled down to keep an eye on the Hunsackers. It didn't seem like they were very much concerned. All they did was squat around in a semicircle with the reins of their horses in their hands and stare his way. The horses looked none too good for the experience, but at least they were able to stand still in each other's shade. The body of the man Longarm had shot lay on the light-colored desert floor. Longarm reckoned he'd swell pretty quick. Longarm looked up in the sky. Already he could see a few buzzards circling well up in the air.

Six o'clock came and went, and then seven. Longarm was beginning to think about having the two women do something about supper when his eye was suddenly caught by a strange sight. It began as a sort of oblong black object outlined against the desert still some two or three miles away. But as he watched, it grew larger and larger and larger. He could tell that it was a wagon being pulled by four mules. It made him give a slight snort of surprise. From what he could tell, Old Man Hunsacker had not jumped off in hot pursuit with no thought of the future as Longarm had originally hoped.

The wagon came on and on, and he saw two of the horsemen mount up and go to meet it. As it neared, Longarm could see that the wagon carried two big barrels, and he was willing to bet his last dollar that they were full of

100

water for horses and the men. In case they didn't have enough, the wagon would make another trip and bring some more. He would also bet that they had plenty of grub and plenty of cartridges. Well, Hunsacker had said, "Let's go in a hurry," but he had also given the order to bring the supplies on out there. No wonder he had fallen back to a better position. Now, he really was in a position to outwait Longarm.

When the wagon arrived, all hands turned out to unload the supplies that it carried. Longarm had been right about the water. It was mostly for the animals. They had brought a big tub, and since the barrels of water were too heavy for the men to handle, they simply set a tub on the prairie next to the wagon, knocked out the bung hole, and let the water spout into the big tub. They brought the horses over two at a time and let them drink. Longarm watched enviously as they unloaded boxes of provisions and enough canvas for a tent to keep off the burning rays of the sun. Hunsacker knew the desert well.

Since Longarm could see that they were occupied with the business of fixing up a camp, he made his way to the buggy and brought out the grub that had been stored there. He went to the cave where the horses were, and told the girls to fix him some supper. They looked at him grudgingly, but Marianne said with a shrug, "Well, all right. We've all got to eat. I guess it doesn't make no never mind, does it?"

"I just hope," Longarm said, "that neither one of you girls are carrying any poison."

Marianne gave him a look. She said, "Honey, we're in the love business, not the killing business that you're in."

Longarm said, "Well, for the first time, we've got the

101

truth. You're not going to claim to be the fiancées any-more?''

She gave him a bland look. She said, ''Can't fiancées be in the love business, Marshal Long?''

He shrugged. ''Just fix supper. It'll be dark in about an hour and a half, and then things might get kind of hot around here.''

Longarm was amused when he got back to his rifle position to see that the Hunsackers had finished their camp. Two tents were pitched. One was nothing but a flat tarpaulin stretched out between poles and anchored with ropes. It did little more than provide shade. It was big enough that the horses could be driven up under it, and now the animals were standing in the relative coolness, eating hay and feed.

The other tent was a big, closed-sided affair, but Longarm could see it was the center of the operation. A campfire had been built. Where they had gotten the wood, Longarm had no idea, but he suspected from the wagon. So far as the wagon went, it and the mules that had drawn it had disappeared. But as he watched, he saw it coming out of a depression in the ground and reappear far off in the distance.

If he had any guess in the matter, he figured the wagon would be going back to replenish the water in the barrels and get more grub and firewood, and then turn around and come back. He swore softly to himself. He didn't much care for this situation as much as he thought he was going to. He rubbed his jaw, feeling the day's growth of whiskers. Things were not going as he had preferred, but then, he didn't know when they ever did.

He had decided that if there was going to be an attack, they would wait until the moon had set somewhere around four o'clock in the morning. It was going to be a long night, and he was the only one on duty. Longarm reckoned he'd just have to forget about sleep. He took one last look at the Hunsacker camp, and then went down the row of rocks and ducked into the cave where the girls were frying ham in a skillet and warming up some of the biscuits they had brought with them.

When it was ready, they put the meal together, but very little was said. Longarm took the occasion to warn the two young women again not to walk across the desert at night, because it could be very dangerous as the Hunsackers were probably going to shoot at any movement. He said, "Yes, you are my bait. I make no bones about it. You're what I've lured the Hunsackers with this far, and if I ain't got you, I ain't got much. But it's a long way to their camp, and a whole bunch of things could happen. Keep that in mind."

The girls hadn't bothered to answer him. He went to where he had dumped his saddle and bedroll, and took out two blankets and the slicker he carried for outdoor use. He carried them back to the two women to pitch on the floor of the cave. "That's the best I can do for you. I don't know what you've got to sleep in, but your luggage is in the buggy. I reckon you can fetch it yourself. I'm going to be kind of busy. I wouldn't be running around the rocks too frisky either, because I am going to be a little nervous and my finger on that trigger could be a little quick."

He left them and went back to his post, not at all satisfied with the way things were going. In the first place, he was good and tired out and he hadn't had much sleep for the last two or three nights. That was going to make staying awake that much harder. He couldn't decide in his mind if

103

he expected an attack that night or not. Likely, they would try to wear him out by just sitting and eating, but when they came, they'd probably come from all sides.

It started out as a long night, and it only got longer. Sometime around ten, the moon came up and he could see the shadows of the rocks that protected him. The moonlight made strange shapes out of the Hunsacker camp. The one advantage was that it was difficult for them to move about without being clearly seen against the white of the desert floor. Fortunately, he had a handy rock that he could sit on while he gazed out through the cleft of the rock wall. His guess was that his greatest vulnerability was behind him and to his left, where the rocks were low and broken. And, of course, the biggest opening was behind him to the north.

He couldn't smoke, but he had brought the bottle of whiskey he had left, and every now and then he took a small nip. If nothing else, it helped him to keep awake. But still, the hours dragged. He looked at his watch at eleven, then at twelve, and then again at twelve-thirty. After that, he resolved that he would just tell time by the stars.

He was tired, more so than he had been in a long time. He was tired physically from running around all over the desert. But he was tired mentally of the game of being a lawman, of hunting desperados like the Hunsackers. It was a twenty-four-hour-a-day job with very few breaks in between. He was sick of this dry country, sick of this lonely country, sick of this desolate country, and especially sick of people like the Hunsackers.

He certainly wished that he was back in Denver with his lady friend who owned the dressmaking shop, back at his favorite saloon at his favorite poker table with some of his good Maryland whiskey in front of him. But unfortunately, there was this little mess to clean up before he could go back and enjoy the comfort of doing a little living for a change instead of merely existing and getting by.

The night ran on. He shifted down from the gun port between the two rocks to a seat almost on the hard floor. He was growing very sleepy, and by the depth of the darkness, he judged it to be at least two o'clock, and maybe even a little later. It didn't really make any difference what time it was. The Hunsackers were now calling the tune on the time.

He sat facing the east side of his fort, the side where the rocks were low, some no more than up to a man's chest. He expected the attack to come from there, though as dark as it was, he doubted that he could do much to defend himself if they tried it and came quietly. But the inside of the rock outcropping was a hard place to be quiet in, since it was full of all kinds of things to trip over and knock against.

In spite of himself, his eyelids were growing heavy. He hoped this would come down to a shooting match before it came down to a sleeping match. If it came down to a sleeping match, he was going to lose. His plan was to wait until daylight, until the desert turned into a frying pan, and then handcuff the girls together or tie them up and catch some sleep, not expecting the Hunsackers to come at such a time.

As he sat, nodding, struggling to hold his eyes open, he suddenly heard a tiny sound. He was instantly alert. He had slumped down against a rock, and was lying almost on his back with one of his shoulders propped up. His rifle was at his side. He let his right hand slip down to his pistol butt. Without opening his eyes, he slowly let them slit a little and looked out though his eyelashes.

Chapter 7

If anything, he smelled her before he recognized her dim form in the night. He started to speak, to ask what she was doing, but from out of the darkness of her form, a hand reached to his mouth and covered it. It was Marianne. At first, when he had caught a glimpse of the movement in the night, he'd only known by the rustle of the skirts that it was a woman. Which one, he couldn't be sure until she came close and he smelled the musky perfume of her body.

Without a word, she reached down and began to unbutton his jeans. The smell of her, the nearness of her, and now her touch brought him instantly erect. He had no idea whatsoever what she was doing or why she was doing it. All he knew was that he wasn't going to fight. He felt her take his member out of the constraints of his jeans, and then he saw her head dip, and felt a warmth go all through him as her mouth enveloped him. He gasped and thrust upward slightly. For a moment, she played with him with her tongue. He started to put his hand on her head, but as if she had anticipated that, she pushed his arm back. He lay back against the rock, panting, the passion taking him and shaking him like a terrier with a rag doll.

When he was so fiery inside that he thought he could no longer stand it, she raised her head and then rose to her knees and straddled his body. With her hands on his chest, she walked her way up until she was positioned over his throbbing penis. She reached under her skirts, and then quickly lowered herself on him. She had planned it well beforehand—she wore no underclothes.

She plunged him inside her. For the next moment, she rolled and rocked and pistoned her body up and down so that her vagina rode his length.

It was over too soon. Suddenly, the world turned bright white before his eyes. The rocks disappeared. The sky disappeared. He arched his back and stared up into the blinding whiteness, shot through with bolts of vivid color. It seemed to last forever, but all too quickly, he slumped back, gasping for breath, panting, spent.

As quickly as she had come, she was gone. Before he could realize what was happening, Marianne had risen to her feet, turned, and was running away. He could hear her gleeful laugh. Over her shoulder, she said, "Now, try and stay awake after that."

Longarm stared at her retreating form. She was right. She had done a good job on him. The first thing a man wanted after such an experience was a nap, and he had already been sleepy well before her visit. Damn her, he thought. But then, he had to smile ruefully. If the woman had thought she had done him a dirty trick, she had another think coming. He could stand those kinds of tricks all night long. With a sigh, he pulled himself back up on the rock.

He felt weak, but he knew it wouldn't be long before his strength returned, and in the meantime, he had a lovely memory to last him the rest of the night.

It was sometime later that he caught a flash of movement out of the corner of his eye. He had repositioned himself on the rock just below his firing hole, and he had seen the flicker some twenty yards to his left. It was the darkest part of the night. The moon was down, the stars were fast retreating, and the sun wouldn't be up for another hour or two. He swung his rifle to his left, holding it loosely chest-high, his eyes trying to search the dim dark recesses of the rocky layout.

He could barely make out the eastern outline of his rocky walls against the dark, black sky. He shifted his eyes back to where he had thought he had seen movement, but now he was not so sure. Vision could play tricks on you at night, especially in the desert. He took a step forward. He was almost convinced that it was either Marianne or Verlene. He said in a low voice, "Marianne?"

The words were barely out of his mouth before there was the roar of a gun and the red-hot flame of a muzzle blast. Instinctively, even as he felt something tug at his side, he dropped to one knee, bringing the hammer back on his rifle. He fired without putting the gun to his shoulder. The shot, following on the sound of the other shot, echoed loud in the thin desert air against the hard faces of the rock. It still seemed to him that he heard something like a moan or a grunt and the soft thud of a bullet striking flesh, but he couldn't be sure.

He stooped, moving as quietly as he could, trying to ignore the pain in his side, and worked his way though the rocks toward the middle of the outcropping where the buggy stood, shafts resting on the ground. He had to stay quiet and figure out the situation. Nobody moved that he could see. He took a half-dozen steps, bending low toward the buggy, and then squatted down before searching the perimeter of his fortress. As far as he could tell, he was still alone.

Finally, he reached the buggy and began a search of his fort. He hid behind one of the buggy's high wheels. Carefully, he traced the outline of the rocks with his eyes from one end to the other.

He was about to look to the west when, again, something caught his attention out of the corner of his eye. He swirled his head back just in time to see a figure standing on the rock, making ready to hop to the next rock and then down to the ground outside the outcropping. Without pause, he levered another shell into the chamber of his rifle, threw the gun to his shoulder, and fired. He saw the man jump into air, leaping to the next rock. It seemed to him that the man suddenly gained momentum, falling and pitching forward more than he jumped. Longarm could not hear the bullet strike, but he thought he had hit the man.

He had no time to speculate on such thoughts. The muzzle blast from his rifle revealed his position, and it was necessary that he move. He went quickly to a big rock about ten yards away. Then he paused and studied the ground around him. There was no motion. There was no sound. There was nothing.

It occurred to him that he would be far better off if he had to stay holed up for any span of time in the cave with the water. He had no time to consider his wound or to make any examination. If his strength began to fade, it would be better that he be hidden in the strong place when that happened.

Taking a chance, he hurriedly made his way to the southern end of the rock wall. He painstakingly searched out the cave where the spring was located. He ducked in under the low entrance and settled himself to the floor just inside the mouth. When his breathing had slowed and it was quiet, he could hear the low gurgle of the water as it came through a fissure in the rock and ran downhill behind him. He inched himself forward until his head was just outside the cave's entrance. That way, he was able to look to the left and right and survey all of the area around his little fortress.

Now, for the first time, he became conscious of his wound. It was beginning to throb. He knew the danger of being wounded so far out in the desert with no medical attention available. Even if the wound was not serious, a man could get gangrene or putrefication and die, or he could bleed to death.

Carefully, Longarm put his hand inside his shirt and felt down along his left side. He found no holes up near his ribs. The wound was just below them. It seemed to be about two inches in from his side. He worked his other hand around and felt his back. There was another hole there. It had been a through-and-through hit. The bullet had hit him in the front and gone out the back. That was lucky. It was also lucky that it hadn't hit a rib, sending broken bits of bone through his body. But his hand felt warm and sticky, and he had no doubt that he was bleeding fairly profusely.

There was no use worrying about it, not then. If he relaxed his guard, another member of the gang would no doubt be ready to take advantage. If Longarm let them start shooting into the cave, he would very shortly have slugs ricocheting all over, and one of them would be bound to hit him.

He wished he had his saddlebags, not for any change of clothes, not even for the extra cartridges that were in there, but mainly for the bottle of Maryland whiskey, standing ready to drink. If he had that whiskey, he'd take a drink and then pour a little in his wound, and then take another drink to kill the pain, and then pour a little more in his wound to kill the gangrene, and then take another drink to kill the pain with the whiskey. Between him and the hole in his side, he figured he could polish off about half of the bottle before daylight.

But that wasn't going to happen. All he could do was be very quiet, very still, and very watchful, and wait until dawn.

The pain, at least, had the effect of driving sleep away from his mind. He had no trouble staying awake and alert as the sun slowly rose beside the desert sand and tipped up into the sky. It was with considerable relief that he saw the night shadows driven from the scattered rocks by the rays of the rising sun. When it was good and up, when he was able to see it over the low rim of rocks to the east, he got carefully to his feet, feeling the sharp pain in his side. He cradled his rifle in the crook of his arm, and stepped out through the mouth of the cave into the clear sunshine. It was still cool this early in the morning.

He took the time to reach in his pocket, take out two shells, and reload them in the magazine of his rifle. He didn't expect any trouble, but then he couldn't be sure. They might still be inside the enclosure.

He stood stock-still, listening for any sound. Other than the faint stir of the wind through the cracks and crevices of the rocks, there was no sound. That was the thing about the desert—you never heard a leaf rustle, a bird sing, or the sound of a horse grunt. The desert meant heat and silence.

He set his hat firmly on his head and tugged at the brim, and then started down to the left to the cave where the young ladies were supposed to be with the horses and his saddlebags and his whiskey, and also where he calculated there should be a body that he had hit the night before. He went slowly, his hand holding his side. As he passed the cave where the girls were, he saw that Marianne was standing in the entrance. She gave him a quick look, and then her eyes settled on his bloody shirt.

She said, "You're hurt!"

He nodded. "Would you mind slipping back in there and getting me that bottle of whiskey out of my saddlebag?"

"Why should I?"

"Because it hurts me to stoop over. Is that a good enough reason, or does it make you happy I can't stoop over?"

Marianne gave him a look, and then ducked back into the dark. He could make out her dim outline and that of Verlene's, and he could smell the horses and hear them rustling around. He needed to take them to water soon.

Marianne brought the whiskey back, and he opened it and had a quick hard pull. He put the cork back in and nodded his head at Marianne, who was studying his face. He limped along by the outside wall to where he thought the shot had come from a few hours earlier. It didn't take much effort to find the body. The man was about where Longarm thought he would be. He was lying on his back with a surprised look on his face, his mouth wide open, his

113

arms bent. The rifle he had been carrying was right beside him. Longarm didn't recognize the man. He wasn't any kin of J.J. Hunsacker that Longarm had seen before.

Longarm reached down and got the man's rifle, and then leaned over and even though it hurt, closed the man's eyes with his fingers. He straightened up, looking down in the heat. The man was going to spoil pretty quick. He could throw him over the rocks that formed the outside walls of the outcropping, but he doubted that he had the strength. Longarm wasn't going to do anything that would cause the blood to start pumping again.

He walked along, carrying the two rifles in one hand and the bottle of whiskey in the other. He went to his gun port, where he could get a good view of the Hunsacker camp. He eased himself gently down on the rock that he had been sitting on, and leaned the rifles against another rock. He looked out into the morning.

The two tents were still there, and he was not too surprised to see the wagon returning in the distance. It appeared that J.J. Hunsacker was settling in for a long siege. What J.J. didn't know, though, was the he had lost one man for sure, and maybe another one, depending on whether that other man had gotten over the wall or had been shot over. Longarm watched for a long time, trying to discern any sign of movement or purpose, but other than a few scattered figures walking around, apparently going about the business of the camp, there was no scheme or plan to be discerned.

He took the bottle of whiskey and had another pull. He slipped down from the rock and lay on his back. He pulled his shirt up in the front and craning his neck, looked down to where the wound was in his side. It was a clean hole, sure enough, and looked about the proper caliber to be at least a .44 or .45. He reckoned the hole in the back was a good deal bigger than the neat little hole in the front.

Gritting his teeth, he took the bottle of whiskey and held it poised over the bloody hole. Then, looking away, he poured the whiskey with shaking hands down into the depth of his own body. He wanted to scream, to gnash his teeth, to bite on a stick. He did nothing but simply endure it. For a minute, he thought he was not going to be able to stand the pain. He poured more in, willing himself to do it. Finally, his hands started to tremble, the whiskey seemed to cauterize the wound, and the pain eased somewhat.

He sat up slowly. After the burn of the whiskey, the pain from the shot itself seemed like nothing. He took another drink out of the bottle, and then shook his head and said, "Whew!" several times out loud before putting the cork back in the bottle and climbing back up on his rock. For a moment, he just sat there quietly, watching the Hunsacker camp, not thinking about anything. He knew he had to go search for the other body, but for the moment, he was in no hurry.

Longarm stood up slowly, feeling pain in his side, and was aware of Marianne coming around the slight bulge in the rock wall, stopping to pause by the dead man, and then coming on to stand in front of him. Longarm said, "Should be lobbing some shells in here directly. I wouldn't be out walking around as free and easy, was I you. I'd get back in that cave and crouch down the best I could."

She wasn't heeding his word. Instead she stared at his bloody shirt. "Let me see that," she said.

He shook his head. His shirt was hanging outside his jeans, but he didn't think it was a sight for a woman's eyes. He said, "I reckon not."

115

Before he could stop her, she had reached over and lifted his shirt, revealing the wound. He saw her face pinch tightly. She looked first at the front and then the back. "At least it's not still lodged inside of you."

Longarm said, "No, it went clean through. It ain't as bad as it looks."

Marianne said, "It's stopped bleeding, but if you go to stirring around much, it's going to start again and you look like you've already lost a lot of blood."

Longarm said, "I reckon it'll be all right."

Without a word, she suddenly leaned over, pulled up her skirt, and ripped and tore a linen undergarment loose. He could see her white petticoat and its lace along the bottom with its smooth cloth falling into fans. Tearing a piece about six inches wide into a square, she put it around the wound at his back. She took his hand and told him, "Hold this."

He did as he was told while she wound the long bandage around him, slipping his fingers out just as she pulled it tight so that the square cloth that she had put over the wound would hold.

When she was done, she stopped back while he held his shirt. "Yes, that ought to help," she said. "Though if you get to jerking around, you'll get to bleeding again, sure as hell."

He said curiously, "Where did you get your nursing skill?"

She shrugged and gave him a look. "I guess when you've been raised in the life I was raised, you get a chance to see a lot of gunshot wounds."

"I'm sorry to hear that."

"What difference does it make?" She jerked her head

back toward the body. "Who is that back there?"

Longarm shook his head. "I don't know his name. In fact, I'm pretty sure I've never seen him before."

She motioned to Longarm's wounds. "Did he do that?"

"I would reckon so. All I saw, though, was a flash of a muzzle blast. Then it hit me. I just fired at the muzzle blast."

She glanced toward the body. It had a bullet hole dead center in the chest. "Must have been a lucky shot."

Longarm smiled slightly. "Well, it put me ahead for the time being, though you could say that we both fired at about the same time. I reckon he came off second best, at least for the time being. There's always the chance before I get out of here that we could end up tied."

Now Marianne gave him a slight smile. "I doubt, Marshal Long, that you are going to leave this desert."

Before he could answer her surprising statement, Marianne turned on her heels and walked back toward the cave, leaving him standing, staring after her. He was about to start her way, following her footsteps, when a heavy slug hit the rock near where he was standing, and then went whining off into the distance, followed almost immediately by a boom. Longarm knew what it was—Jim Stock with his Sharps heavy-caliber rifle. That was going to make moving around the compound a little chancier than it had been. Longarm ducked down and hurried toward the cave with the water. He wanted to get a good drink before he started out to find what had happened to the second man who had infiltrated their premises the night before.

Chapter 8

It didn't take long to find the body. The man had fallen down between two big rocks. Longarm located him easily enough, but had difficulty getting into a position to see the man's face. He looked familiar, and Longarm was fairly certain it was one of J.J. Hunsacker's kin, but whether he was a son or a cousin of the old man, Longarm didn't know for sure. The man looked young, in his mid-twenties maybe, and he was wearing a side arm and carrying a shotgun. Longarm was considerably surprised at the shotgun. Apparently they had expected to do some close-in work. Maybe the old man knew about the caves, and thought that was the best way to clear out one of them.

There was nothing that Longarm could do about the second dead man either. He doubted that he could manhandle both bodies over the outer outcropping of rock, even if he hadn't been hurt. As it was, there was nothing to do but leave them where they lay.

As he trudged back across the center of the circle of

rocks, there came the whizz of a heavy slug as it passed through the air, and then a boom. The bullet hit the northern wall of rocks, glanced off, and then whizzed and whined almost through the center of the camp. Longarm heard the slug strike near one of the cave's entrances. It was clear that J.J. Hunsacker had Jim Stock throwing in enough lead to keep him nervous. It was unlikely that the random shots would do much harm, but it kept the body tense, just waiting for the next one.

Longarm hurried across the floor of the little fortress, and made his way to the cave where the girls and the horses were hiding. He had left his bottle of whiskey down by his firing port when Marianne had made him the bandage. He'd also left the rifle of the first dead man. It was a slightly larger caliber than Longarm's .44 weapon. Longarm guessed it to be a .44-60, the latter number referring to the powder load. To Longarm's mind, that was a light powder load for a .44-caliber weapon, but it did give him an idea. He had taken the shotgun shells from the second dead man, but he hadn't taken the shotgun. At that moment, he had no need for the gun. For any close work that he'd ever needed done, Longarm had used his revolver.

He bypassed the cave, even though he saw Marianne's face peering out at him. He could hear the shuffle and movement of the horses and the mule. He passed the dead man again, and got back down to his firing slot. Before he did anything, he had another drag from his bottle of whiskey. It was already beginning to get hot, and the whiskey was warming up accordingly.

Longarm peered around the cleft in the rock toward the Hunsackers' camp. It had seemed to him that Jim Stock's shot had come from a little higher vantage point, and he was startled to see that Stock had taken a position on the wagon and that they had built him some kind of a perch. It didn't raise the man more than ten or twelve feet above the desert floor, but the angle was an advantage in shooting into the rock enclosure. Even as he looked, Longarm saw a white puff of smoke and heard the whizzing ricochet of the big slug that Stock was firing out of his .50-caliber rifle, followed by a boom.

Longarm stared thoughtfully, thinking about the man perched up on that high handmade stool they had built for him on the back of the wagon. He got one of the cartridges out of the magazine of the dead man's rifle, and then, with the point of the knife, he worked the slug out of the brass casing. There was a wad inside, which he carefully picked out with his knife.

After that, he set the brass casing down so that the powder wouldn't leak out, and opened a shotgun shell he had selected. He poured out the pellets, pulled out the wad, and looked down into the flecks of powder that remained. Holding the shotgun shell casing in his right hand and the rifle cartridge in the other, he slowly added some of the shell's powder into the cartridge. He added as much as he dared.

What he was about to do was a rather dangerous trick. The manufacturer decided how much powder to put in a cartridge. If you put more in, you could very well have gun blow up in your face. Longarm had seen several examples of that, and it hadn't been pretty.

When he was through adding the powder, he replaced the plug in the rifle cartridge, and then took the lead slug and rammed it home so that it was in place. Now, except for the added powder, the .44-60 cartridge was as good as new. He slid the action back on the man's rifle, and inserted

121

the cartridge with the extra powder into the chamber. Then he rammed the mechanism closed and swung the rifle around, aiming it out the little cleft in the rocks. If he had been smart, and if he was very, very lucky, the extra powder would give the slug enough carry to reach Jim Stock, who was sitting on his perch on the wagon.

Longarm sighted carefully along the rifle's length, calculating the distance, the lack of wind, and how much the slug would drop in such a distance. He finally settled on a point about six feet over Jim Stock's head. He let out his breath, and then slowly squeezed the trigger. The rifle slammed against his shoulder, and the boom almost deafened him. For an instant, Longarm thought that the muzzle had exploded, but no such thing had happened. Even as he blinked from the severe kick of the rifle, he saw Stock suddenly throw his arms up into the air and then fall backwards. He couldn't tell if he had hit the man or not. Stock had fallen hard, but he had hit behind the wagon and Longarm couldn't see. The shot brought an instant volley of lightweight carbine fire from the Hunsacker camp. It was ineffective, some of the cartridges not even reaching the rock walls, the others glancing harmlessly away from the rock and falling into the sand.

Longarm picked up his own rifle, and then hurriedly made his way as fast as the pain in his side would let him back to the cave with the water. He got down on his hands and knees and took a long drink. It was very easy to get thirsty in such conditions, but he was more than thirsty. The plain fact of the matter was that he was worried. Longarm didn't like the way the situation was developing. It didn't matter whether he had hit Jim Stock or not. Stock's rifle would still be there, and any one of the half-dozen men left in the camp could fire it.

Longarm stood up from the springs and turned toward the entrance, wondering in his mind what steps he would take to get out of the plight he found himself in. It didn't seem that he was chasing the Hunsackers now as much as being chased. Just as he took a step toward the entrance of the cave, Marianne appeared in the lighted opening.

With the sun shining behind her, her hair looked even brighter and more golden than before. She looked at him as he came up to her, tilting her head to look up into his face. "Marshal Long, what are you going to do? I've had a look out there, and it appears to be that Mr. Hunsacker is just a little more than serious about this. The man doesn't like to be shamed and showed up in front of his woman and his kinfolks, especially his sons."

Longarm tried to act unconcerned. "Oh, I don't see where there's been any showing up on my part. It appears to me that I'm the one inside this rock jail. He's out there with all the grub and all the water and all the ammunition. Plus he's got plenty of reinforcements. I'm not expecting any myself."

Marianne said, "Maybe you think it's funny now, but you're not going to think it's so funny if you spend another night without sleep. You can't afford to sleep."

Longarm nodded his head slowly. "No, but I appreciate the way you woke me up last night."

She grimaced suddenly. "That was mean of me and I admit it," she said. "I shouldn't have done that, but Verlene and I got to talking and it seemed funny at the time. Besides that, I was very angry with you. You stopped us from a lawful pursuit, and you had no right to do that."

"Maybe I did and maybe I didn't, Miss Marianne. I can't account for what you think I have to do. What I can account for is how I do my job. That's all I've done from the very beginning. I've tried to do my job as a peace officer for the United States Government. Maybe it ain't in line with what you think I ought to be doing, but I don't answer to anybody except my boss, and he ain't here. He's back in Denver."

Marianne said, "Whether you think you're right or wrong doesn't make much difference. I'm telling you, Marshal Long . . ."

"Deputy Long, please."

"All right, if it's that important. Deputy Long. I'm telling you, Deputy, that wound looks bad. You are weakened, haven't had any sleep, and we're very low on food. Verlene and I have both taken our breakfast, and there's enough left for your breakfast and for one more meal today. I don't know what we'll do after that. You know, if that wound gets infected, you're going to be in real trouble. Now, what I think . . . well, never mind what I think."

"No, let me hear."

She looked out toward the opening at the scattered rocks at the center of the enclosure. Just then another heavy slug slammed against the rock, with the sound of another heavy boom. Apparently, Longarm thought, he hadn't silenced Jim Stock after all.

"I think you should get on your horse, take the other one with you, and ride toward Reno," said Marianne. "That miners camp is off in that direction." She pointed to the northwest. "About three miles. At least I think it is. I'm not all that certain, and I don't know what kind of a welcome you'd get. If your horses are in good shape, I think you should try for Reno. I think you need help, a doctor or something.''

Longarm smiled. ''That's good of you to think about me, Miss Marianne. I couldn't rightly leave you out here in the middle of this desert.''

She said dryly, ''Oh, I don't think we'd be alone long. But I do think it would give you time enough to get a head start where they couldn't catch you before you could get back to some sort of civilization. We would give you a good hour or so before we signaled them to come forward.''

Longarm said, ''Why don't you signal them anyway? That would solve all my problems. If you get them within fifty yards of this rock pile, I guarantee you all my troubles would be over. I don't know about yours.''

Marianne stiffened and glared at him. ''Are you insinuating that I would betray my friends?''

Longarm gave her a mocking look. ''Miss Marianne, who do you think you're fooling? The Hunsackers are not friends of yours. This is all a business proposition. I know it and you know it. Why don't you admit it? Look, you're a decent enough woman—you've already showed me that side of you. Why don't you go all the way and be decent all around. I'd like to see you from the other side.''

She turned on her heel and marched out of the cave. Longarm followed her, and then stopped suddenly as another slug came whining into the enclosure. It came nowhere near him, but it was unnerving. After a few moments, he walked out onto the desert floor, and then turned left and traveled a few yards to the main cave. It was time for some sort of breakfast, but before that, he wanted to get one more look at the Hunsackers to make sure they weren't up to anything.

It required a little climbing, but he took it carefully so as not to put any great strain on his side. He was able to peer out between two rocks. The sun was up good now, and in a little while, he wouldn't be able to put his bare hands on the big rocks. He would blister his palms. He could already feel the heat pounding on his back like a waterfall, but it didn't seem to be bothering J.J. Hunsacker and his brood.

They all seemed to be back, in under the big tent they had thrown up, leaving the sides off to let what breeze there was come through. The only person out in the sun was someone who had taken Jim Stock's perch high up on the little platform they had built.

As Longarm watched, he saw the man aim for a long time and then fire. He saw the flash of smoke, and then heard the whine of the bullet before the sound reached his ear. He guessed that it was a game they were going to continue to play, just to keep the women unsettled maybe.

He reckoned that Minnie Sewell would have filled J.J. Hunsacker in with all the peculiarities about Longarm's situation with the two young women. Old J.J. wouldn't be too worried about Longarm fooling around with the ladies. But that wouldn't keep him from urgently being pestered by his sons into fetching them into their beds.

Longarm studied the layout for a few moments, watching to make sure that no daylight raids were being planned. For now, it seemed that the Hunsackers were content to rest their horses under the shade of the tent, and to rest themselves and to drink whatever they had. As carefully as he could, Longarm clambered down from the rocks and then made his way into the cave, carrying his Winchester with him.

The women had found a way to heat some beans, and there was a good portion of them left. They had made a little fire from some dried wood that they'd found. He sat down beside them, and Marianne silently make him a plate of beans and dried beef. There was no bread of any kind left. He was aware of his side as he ate, but he tried to ignore it. Verlene looked at him with hard eyes, but Marianne almost seemed sympathetic as she handed him a tin cup of cold water and shook her head. "How's your wound?"

He said, "It ain't bothering me overmuch."

Verlene said, "You're a lucky old sonofabitch. You should be dead."

Longarm sighed and said, "Verlene, I'm no sonofabitch. I know that. But you ain't got to remind me that I'm old."

She said, "Go to Hell."

Marianne hadn't been far from wrong when she'd said they were going to run out of food and run out of it quick. As he ate, he reflected on the fact that J.J. Hunsacker would know how much food they had left. He should. He had been the one who'd sent it down by Minnie Sewell.

While he was eating, Verlene looked at Longarm with her hard eyes. She said, "You're a damned fool. You better run while you've got the chance. Marianne said that we'd hold up on giving the alarm to let you get a head start. She can speak for herself. I'm not sure I want to do that."

Longarm shook his head. "I didn't expect you would, Verlene. There's a lot of money to be made off that crowd, and I imagine that you'll try for every penny."

Marianne said wearily, "Don't you two start at each

other. This is a fix that none of us are enjoying. It's hot as hell. I haven't had a bath in I don't remember when. The food is horrible.'' She looked first at Longarm and then at Verlene. "And the company is even worse.''

Longarm had expected to feel better once he had eaten, but it hadn't seemed to work. He felt as weak as he had earlier that morning. Every once in a while, a little chill would run through him and then he would feel hot. He finished his meal with a can of peaches, opening the top with his pocketknife, and then spearing the peaches with the blade and eating them straight out of the can. After that, he crinkled the can and poured the juice straight down his throat. It was sweet and good, and he hoped it would give him some strength.

He got up and said, "Ladies, it's about time I got back to work. You be thinking about what you can do to help me get out of this fix.''

Both of the girls gave him a look that was intended to wither the shirt on his back, but he just shrugged it off. He had been joking. Apparently they hadn't been in a joking mood. He wondered what his boss, Billy Vail, would do if he were in this situation. Well, that was easy to answer. The reason Billy Vail was boss was that he didn't get himself into such situations. The way to avoid this sort of mess was to not get in it in the first place.

Longarm took a moment to look the horses over. They seemed to be fine, but the mule still looked a little down. Longarm would have to come back a little later in the morning or early afternoon, and take them back down to the cave and give them a drink of water. He gave the two young women a final nod, and then ducked through the entrance and walked slowly down to his rifle position.

The day dragged by slowly. Several times, he walked down to fill himself up with water. It seemed the sun dried him out about ten minutes faster than he could fill up. Once, he took the horse and the mule to the stream and let them drink their fill. They had been rested long enough that they could be trusted with the water. After that, he put them away and then had a drink of his whiskey.

Neither one of the young women paid him much of a mind, but it seemed to him that Marianne gave him a good looking over. Once Verlene said, "What are we supposed to do? Just sit around here and wait for them to kill you so that we can get along with our business?"

Longarm had an answer, but he just shook his head and went on out.

The sun got straight overhead at noon, and then slowly began to drop toward the west. It was very difficult for him to hold his eyes open. Occasionally, his chin would drop on his chest and he would nap for five or ten minutes at a stretch. He was the kind who could do such a thing and not wake up either dead or somebody's prisoner. If he was going to sleep, he knew it was best done during the hottest part of the day when the Hunsackers were content to stay in the comfort of their tent. But truthfully, he did not know how much longer he could last. He was nearly out of whiskey, nearly out of food, and completely out of sleep. If it had not been for the driving desire that was built into his very fiber to catch the men he'd started after, he would have abandoned the chase and gone after help.

The light chills caught him now and again. He was hot enough so it was impossible to tell if he was running any fever, but he had had infections before and he knew the symptoms. He took a look at his wounds from time to time, but they didn't seem to be any redder or any angrier than when he had first been shot. He was moving around enough to keep from getting stiff, but not enough to cause any fresh discharge of blood.

About six o'clock by his watch, he went back down to the cave and had another meal of beans and beef. It wasn't very good, but it was filling.

Marianne said, "We've just a little meat left, and the cheese and a few canned goods—tomatoes, peaches, and whatnot. After that, it's all gone."

Longarm said, "You can always go out and stand with your mouth open and let the moon shine on your tongue. I've heard moonlight was right filling."

Verlene said, "Oh, don't try and be joking, Marshal. You're not the man for the job."

Longarm said mildly, "I thought you were sort of prickly when we first met, but I do think you are getting more and more thorny. Pretty soon, a man won't be able to get within five feet of you without feeling a sharp stab."

For answer, she just looked away.

Longarm walked back to his post. There was only about an hour of daylight left. He felt pretty good at the moment, but he didn't know how much longer that would last.

It gradually grew dark, and the desert became painted with moonshine as the big orb slowly rose in the heavens. Longarm paid the Hunsackers careful attention. He would not put it past J.J. to try and pull something just when Longarm was least expecting it. He carefully counted the number of horses under the tent, and got a fair count of the number of men. It looked to be about the right number. He had no reason to believe that anyone had cut out to the east or the west to try and flank him during the night by coming up from his blind side. But then he didn't really have a blind side, not from his position. Now that the moon was up, anyone who tried to ride away from the Hunsackers' camp would be in full view. Other than a direct frontal attack, his only danger lay in falling asleep.

Longarm watched until his eyes ached. He had his whiskey with him, and he was taking little nips every now and then.

Longarm could tell that he was suffering from an infection. The chills were coming closer and closer together, and he could feel the fever building up in his body, even in the heat. Most worrisome were the red streaks running away from his wounds. He knew what that meant. The wounds had somehow gotten corrupted, and he hadn't figured out a way to get the corruption out of his body before he got too weak to help himself. The problem was that doing what was necessary would leave him even weaker.

He looked up at one point, and Marianne was standing there, studying him. She said, "You're sick, aren't you?"

He said, "No." He shook his head. He didn't think it was wise for either one of the women to know how bad off he was. "No, I'm fine." He tried to make his voice strong. "Why would you want to go and think a thing like that?"

Marianne came closer. "Because it's all over your face. That wound has done got infected, hasn't it?"

He shook his head again. "I don't know what you're talking about. I'd know if it was infected."

"Let me see it."

"Listen, dammit. It ain't none of your affair. I ain't asking for no nurse and I'm not looking to get one. Right now, you're in my custody, so you do what I tell you."

She suddenly knelt by his side and lifted his shirt. She said with a low whistle, "Oh, yes. That's bad. You're going to have to open that up or you're not going to make it."

He jerked his shirt out of her hand. "Don't be tending to no business that ain't your own, Marianne. This ain't your business."

She looked at him with surprising compassion. "Deputy Long, I'm not near as bad a person as you think I am. I know you think that I'm a common whore, and I know you think I am against the law. But I don't care to see a man suffer when something can be done about it. As I've told you, I've had some hand at tending the sick, and not just because of my line of work."

He said, nodding his head toward the Hunsackers' camp, "I don't reckon we'd have much time to do surgery in here with that bunch of vultures out there waiting to swoop down."

She said as she stood up, "You might as well face it, Deputy Long. They have the upper hand. The best thing you could do would be to make the hard ride to safety. I think you can get to someplace where you would be safe and could open your wound and let it drain. You need to be well before you go after Mr. Hunsacker and his sons. You're no match for them now."

He licked his dry lips. "I reckon you're right. That would give you a chance to go on about your business. I reckon you'd like that."

She shook her head slowly. "No, I was planning on going with you to take care of you and help you with what needs to be done."

It startled him so, he couldn't speak for a moment. He

said, "Go with me? Leave this sure money?" He jerked his head again toward the Hunsackers' camp. "Ain't your fiancé over there waiting for you with a fistful of double eagles?"

She said, "It never was what you thought. There are some things that I don't charge for, and this is one of them. I think you'd better consider that we could slip away during the night. You had better think seriously about it."

He shook his head as if to clear the cobwebs. He said, "What about the other young lady? Verlene? What does she say?"

"Verlene is not very smart. Verlene is perfectly placed for what she knows. She's not very fond of you, Deputy Long. I think she'll stay here, but as soon as they come in, she'll tell them where you have gone. That's why I think we should wait until she's asleep and then slip out."

Longarm sat there, studying her for a full moment. He said, "I don't know what to make of all this. I've got to give it some thought. You're right about one thing. I do have an infection. I've got the chills and the fever and everything that goes with it."

She motioned with her hand. "It doesn't take a very sharp eye to see that you are not far from something even more serious than an infection."

"Are you talking about gangrene?"

She nodded. "What do you think? How long does it take in this heat?"

"You go on back now to the cave. I'll let you know something soon."

She nodded, and started back over the rock-strewn desert floor. Longarm let her take several steps before he called her name. She turned. He said, "Whichever way it turns out, Marianne, I want to thank you for the offer. That was mighty kind of you.''

She shrugged her shoulders. "Forget it, Deputy Long. I'd do it for anyone.''

He half smiled. "Well, then. I won't go getting a big head thinking that I've been treated special by a pretty lady.''

It brought a half smile to her face. She said, "Yes, that's right. Don't feel special.''

After it got good and dark, he changed his firing position, clambering painfully and slowly up a pile of rocks to a much higher vantage point. He was about fifteen or twenty yards above the desert floor, and he could see clearly. The moon hid behind clouds, but he could make out the dark figures around the Hunsackers' camp.

He was no more than settled with his rifle in position when, to his surprise, he saw two men swing aboard their horses and start off to the east. He could not tell where they were headed because they never veered toward him. He saw them ride over a slight rise in the desert floor, and then watched as they disappeared as if the ground had swallowed them.

After that, all he could do was sit and watch toward the direction the men had taken. There was nothing out there. There was no town, there was no well, there was nothing. It was his guess that they were going to swing far to the east and then come back, perhaps from the north or northeast, in hopes of coming through the north entrance of the enclosure.

Longarm sat, thinking about it, studying the desert, waiting to see if the men would appear at some other location. If he were to proceed on his assumption that they were going to try to flank him, he would be leaving himself unprotected from the other sides. He didn't know what else to think. He hated the idea of climbing back down the rock and then making his way across the enclosure to meet the possible threat, but he hated even worse the thought of trying to fend off an attack from his rear.

Just as he started to move, the thought came that might be exactly what Hunsacker was counting on him to think, and that the real attack would come through the western opening. He slid down as best he could to be out of sight, yet still be able to keep an eye on the Hunsacker camp. If they were coming, they should come fairly quickly. They would assume that he would take the bait and move his defense to meet them, leaving the western opening unguarded.

There was no way to know exactly what they were going to do. J.J. Hunsacker had never struck Longarm as the smartest hombre around. In the last gunfight they had had, Hunsacker had made some bad mistakes. He had sacrificed some men but, Longarm thought, had gotten away with himself and most of his close family. The men he had sacrificed had been some third cousins and hangers-on and such. It had been a bloody gunfight, but none of the blood that had been spilled had been close to J.J. Hunsacker.

Longarm wondered if the two men he had seen riding off to the east were a couple of decoys to be picked off at no cost to J.J. while the near and dear ones attacked from the west. He shook his head. It was going to be a tough, long wait and a tough decision. Two men had gotten inside the night before, and they had come from the east. More reason to think that that would be the direction they would come from again, but Longarm still doubted it.

His main problem now was where to locate himself. If a party left the Hunsacker camp and rode to the west, he would not be able to see them from his previous position. The only position from which he could see with any clarity was the high perch he was presently occupying, but it was too far from the western entrance to do him any good in a gunfight. He didn't want anybody getting inside the rock enclosure. He wanted to stop them at least a hundred yards away. He said softly, "Damn, damn, damn." It was a hell of a time to be feeling bad, but there was nothing else for him.

He cursed softly under his breath as he made his way down from the high place, almost stumbling once or twice, catching himself in time. Once on the desert floor, he walked to a place beyond his former gun position, a place where he could see to the west, although his vision was badly restricted toward the south and the Hunsacker camp. It was the best firing position he could find if the attack came from the west or the north. He knew there was no way to be sure. All he could do was go on his best instincts.

Longarm settled down and began searching the desert. The moon still hadn't come all the way up, and if anything, it was still fairly dark. He looked at his watch. The best he could see, it was somewhere around eight o'clock. In another half hour, the moon would be high. If they were going to circle him, now would be the time.

Almost as if on order, several riders suddenly appeared passing the thin cracks in the rocks to the west. They crossed his line of vision. He stood up and hurried to a place that faced south, in their direction. Once there, he took off his hat and lifted his head slightly above the boulders. He could see three men distinctly now. They were swinging wide to the west, and even as he watched, they were turning back toward his fortress. They were going to attack him.

As he saw the men start to come toward his position, he heard gunfire from the east. Rifles cracked and bullets splattered into the rocks. The two men who had ridden to circle him were now positioned out in the desert, attempting to draw his attention away from the three Hunsacker men who were making a serious advance.

Longarm could see the three begin to spread out as they rode slowly toward the opening in the rock walls. Behind him, the firing continued, but he paid it no mind. As long as they wanted to stand out in the desert and shoot slugs into the rocks, that was all right by him. He was more interested in the business of the three he was watching.

He calculated they were some seven or eight hundred yards away, a half mile at the most. They had topped the rise in the desert floor and then dropped down into a depression. They kept on coming, steadily, aiming at the big break in the rock on the western side. They were riding with about ten yards distance between each man, but it was gradually narrowing down as they rode closer. They had their horses in a fast walk.

He expected them, when they were close enough, to make a dash to get inside the fort and blaze away at anything that moved and wasn't wearing a skirt. He supposed that he could go and get Verlene and use her for cover, but that hardly seemed the gentlemanly thing to do. Not that he expected the Hunsackers to act much like gentlemen either.

As he waited, he put his hand inside his shirt and felt the flesh around his bandaged wound. He could tell it was warm, as if it had fever in it, and he could also tell the skin was stretching taut. There was an infection inside him. He had not allowed the wound to heal from the inside out as he was supposed to. Instead, the holes had closed up on the outside, keeping the corruption inside. He had made a mistake. He should have put a little rag in each wound.

The drain rag was called a tent. It tickled him that they should have such a name. There were the Hunsackers out in the desert, taking shade and ease and comfort under a tent. Now, he was distinctly uncomfortable because he hadn't used a tent in his wound. He should have put one piece of rag in each opening to drain it. He was getting careless. The wound had been worse than he had originally thought. He could feel the chills and fever running through him, and he knew he could not hold his present position much longer.

Now the men were about four hundred yards away, and they were picking their horses up into a trot. Longarm assumed that they didn't want to go into a galloping charge just yet because their horses were probably not in good shape, even though they were getting plenty of water. Traveling around in the desert was hard on both a man and his horse, not to mention women.

He slid his rifle across the rock in front of him and sighted on the middle rider. He couldn't tell who it was, but he doubted it was LeeRoy or Joe or Shank, though he would have liked to eliminate Shank as early as possible. He knew for certain that it wasn't the old man. The old man wasn't going to be trotting around the desert at night with bullets aimed at him. He would be back at the camp with a bottle of good whiskey and the ministrations of Minnie Sewell. The old man was probably well on his way to getting his ashes hauled.

Longarm felt a flutter in his stomach as the men got closer. They were preparing themselves for a charge. He guessed them to be no more than 120 or 130 yards away, and any moment now, they would start their horses into a gallop, which would make his first shot that much harder. They rode fearlessly secure, he guessed, figuring that his attention was occupied on the east side of the outcropping. He drew a bead in the center of the middle man's chest. Longarm watched as the dark form got bigger and bigger in his sight. He slowly eased the hammer back on his rifle. They were less than a hundred yards away now, and he could see them lifting their horses into a lope. Longarm waited ten seconds, holding his breath. Then he fired, feeling the kick of his rifle against his shoulder. The middle man disappeared as if a giant hand had slapped him out of the saddle.

That did not deter the other two. They flung themselves further forward on their horse's necks, and kicked the animals up into a gallop, racing fast to the gate. Longarm knew that once they were inside the enclosure, there would be trouble. He tracked the man closest to him, leading him just slightly. The man was so melded into his horse that it was going to be difficult to hit the man and not the horse. Longarm fired, and saw both horse and man go down. He could see the man tumbling free. Longarm jacked another shell into the chamber of his rifle, and fired at the man just as he stood up. He saw the man stagger backwards, and then fall.

He didn't know if he had killed him or not. He had no time to wait. The third man was going to be inside any second. He levered another shell into the chamber, and rose and started toward an opening in the rock to get a head-on shot. He was late. The rider came through the gate, a pistol in his right hand. He fired at Longarm, and in that instant, Longarm fired back. They both missed. Longarm chambered another shell, fell to one knee, and fired again as the man fought to control his horse on the rocky ground. The shot took the man high up on the chest, short of his neck. He went sideways over the side of his horse. Longarm saw him almost bounce as he hit the ground. The riderless horse ran on, trailing the reins, startled and nervous by the gunfire and tripping on rocks. Longarm could hear the clank of a shod hoof as the horse tried to find a way out of the noise and violence. Longarm understood how the animal felt. He didn't care much for it himself.

There was no time to lose. Longarm went quickly to the man's side and leaned down and looked at him. He didn't know him other than he could see the Hunsacker face on him. The man was dead, there was no mistaking that. Longarm took the man's rifle and his side arm, sticking his revolver in his belt.

He walked quickly toward the east side to see what kind of threat the two other men posed. They were still wasting ammunition recklessly. He had knocked down three more of the Hunsacker gang in a short time. The odds were getting better and better. He would like it even more if he could put a dent in the two that were trying to get at him from the east.

Longarm went to the north end of the low rocks, and leaned down and peered up and over. He could just distinguish the two men against the dark sky. They were sitting on their horses some five hundred yards away and methodically pumping round after round into the enclosure. He figured it was going to take luck to score a hit on either man. He decided his best chance was to concentrate on one of the figures and fire rapidly at that one man. Perhaps he could hit the man. Perhaps he would hit the horse. It was not possible for his weapon to make an accurate shot at such a distance.

He eased the hammer back on his carbine and aimed at the man on the left, who was more heavyset than the other. Longarm thought that made him a better target. He fired, smelling the acrid powder as it blasted out from his rifle. He fired again, then three times, then four times, then five. He saw the man's horse go down. He didn't know if he had just hit the horse or the man.

Then the man stumbled free, and Longarm could see him running toward his fellow rider, running heavily across the sand floor of the desert. Longarm fired the single shot left in his rifle at the man, but he didn't break stride. His companion was coming back for him, turning his horse and reaching down to help the stout man get up behind him to ride double.

Frantically, Longarm reached into his shirt pocket and grabbed a handful of cartridges. As quickly as he could, he shoved four of them into the magazine, levered a shell into the chamber, and fired at the men and the horse as the heavyset man tried to get up behind the other man. On his third shot, Longarm saw both men suddenly fall. The second rider looked down at his companion, and Longarm snapped a shot off at him, but he knew it had gone wide. The rider paid no more attention to the man on the ground. Longarm could only guess that the fallen bandit was either badly hurt or dead. The rider spurred his horse and headed straight back for the Hunsackers' camp.

Longarm got up slowly. He walked, methodically loading his carbine. It was about time to get out of this place. If he stayed much longer, he would be dead. He noticed the riderless horse standing in the middle of the fort. He walked to the animal, which was trembling from all the shooting and the noise. He took the horse by the bridle and led him behind him. The least he could do for the animal was let him have a drink of water. The horse followed Longarm to the cave with the bubbling spring.

Longarm led him further into the cave, and watched as the horse immediately went to water. He smelled at the water for several seconds, and then Longarm watched the horse raise his head, water dripping from his jaws before plunging his mouth back in. Longarm didn't know what he was going to do with the third horse, but he didn't see any point in leaving it behind for the Hunsackers.

He led the horse out of the cave and dropped his reins, letting him stand near the wall. Longarm walked down to where the women and his other two horses were. The two girls were standing against the cave wall. They turned quickly as he came in. Marianne said, "What happened? We heard shooting!" She held her hand to her mouth.

Longarm was about to speak when Verlene said with venom in her voice, "Any chance you got shot again, Deputy Long?"

Longarm gave her half a smile. "Sorry to disappoint you, Verlene. There were some people that got shot, but I wasn't one of them this time. Reckon I just got lucky."

Marianne said, looking at him, to his surprise, with concern on her face, "You're all right then?"

He nodded. "Yes, ma'am. Thank you very much. I'm doing pretty well." He walked on to where the two horses were standing, one still bearing the saddle but with the cinch loosened, but still bridled, and the other with a halter and a lead rope. He caught up the bridles and the lead rope and turned. He said, "I reckon I'm going to have to disappoint you, ladies. I'll be pulling my freight."

Marianne said, "You leaving?"

He nodded again. "Yes, I reckon it's about time I got out of here." He gave her a look he knew she would understand. "I don't think I'm going to hold up much longer."

Verlene gave him a hard laugh. "So, you're going to run, are ya? They run you out? I knew they would. I knew all that big, brave lawman talk was just so much stuffing."

Marianne gave her an annoyed look, and said, "That's not necessary, Verlene. Leave the man alone. He's just doing his job."

Verlene looked at her with her mouth open. She said, "When did you go defending the law?"

"I'm not defending the law. The man's hurt. Can't you see that?"

"Maybe you forgot, but he's the man who has held us here against our will, draggin' us halfway around the country."

Longarm said, touching his hand to the brim of his hat, "Well, if you ladies will forgive me, I'm going to get on along. Now, Miss Verlene, I know you're right anxious for the Hunsackers to get their hands on me. But I don't think they're going to be coming up here until dawn, and I don't think it would be a very good idea for you to think about trying to get down to their camp. I might have to hit you on the head with a rock, that kind of thing.''

Verlene drew herself up. ''Did you hear that, Marianne? Hit me on the head with a rock!''

Marianne said, ''Don't be silly, Verlene. He won't hit you with a rock.'' Then she turned her head toward Longarm. ''I'm going with you.''

Longarm frowned slightly. ''Marianne, are you sure that you want to do that?''

''I don't think you can make it without me.''

He grimaced. ''I hate to admit that.''

She said, ''Somebody is going to have to open that wound up. I've never seen anybody who could open a wound in their own self.''

Longarm said, ''I kind of have to agree with you, though I don't see how it's going to make you any too popular with the folks back there.''

Verlene broke in to say, ''Marianne, are you crazy? You can't run out on this deal. There's a lot of money involved here. Minnie has already set it up. All we have to do is wait until this fool is out of here and it will be all right.''

Marianne said, with a touch of anger in her voice, ''Verlene, can't you ever think of anything other than cash? You don't really want to get married, do you? Besides, this deputy here has thinned out the Hunsacker bunch so that I don't think they're going to be so anxious for you and me. I think they are going to be more anxious to find *him*.'' She looked at Longarm when she said it. ''I don't think they'll be stopping for fun. I think they'll be trailing him too fast.''

Longarm nodded. ''Yes, that's why I want to get as much of a start as I can.'' He glanced at Verlene. ''That's why I don't think you better try and get down to their camp tonight. They are liable to shoot you in the dark—not knowing who you are. Or I might shoot you from this side. You might just think I've gone.''

Marianne said sternly, ''I won't have that kind of talk, Deputy Long.''

Longarm gave her a smile. ''My friends call me Longarm.''

Marianne said, ''Well, I ain't your friend, Deputy Long. Hadn't we better get going?''

Longarm nodded. ''I reckon so.'' All he felt was weak. He led the two horses out of the cave, leaving Verlene standing there, with Marianne trailing behind him. He could hear Verlene as she implored Marianne not to do what she was about to do. He heard her say, ''Have you gone crazy in this heat?''

Marianne said, ''The man is wounded. He needs help. If they catch him, they will kill him. He needs someone to help him treat his wounds. It's part of me, Verlene. I don't expect you to understand. Maybe you haven't noticed, but I've never really been a whore. You're a whore, I'm not. I just fuck sometimes for money.''

Longarm could hear the fury in Verlene's voice. She said, ''Why, you bitch. Who the hell do you think you're talking to? You ain't so highfalutin. I've seen you work. Don't try and fool me. Don't you think I won't tell Mr. Hunsacker what you've done, and when he catches up with you and that no good lawman, you'll find out just how high and mighty you are.''

Longarm called back. ''Marianne, if you're going with me, you'd better step it up. The time's getting short.''

Marianne said to Verlene, ''I wouldn't advise you to try and get to Mr. Hunsacker. I'd let him come to you. The marshal told you that there's going to be some itchy trigger fingers around that camp. If you go to slipping up there, you're liable to get the surprise of your life, and it may be the last surprise you ever get.''

She turned and followed after Longarm as he led the two horses to where the third one was standing. There really wasn't much to take. He sent Marianne to fill the big canteen, and then he watered the other two horses even though they had just been watered a few hours earlier. They were going to be traveling across the desert, and they would need all the help they could get.

Longarm was cinching up the saddle on the big bay when Marianne came back. He'd ride the bay for as long as he could, then switch to the smaller, less durable roan. He didn't know anything about the horse he had acquired from the Hunsackers. Marianne would ride that one, and her light weight should keep the animal going at a moderate pace along with his. The horse was a good-looking buckskin, four or five years old, Longarm reckoned. The fact that he was a good-blooded horse made Longarm think that whoever had been on his back had been a son rather than a cousin to old J.J. A fine horse like that would naturally go to one of his sons.

Longarm helped Marianne up on the buckskin. She didn't need much assistance. He gave her a little lift to help her get her small slipper in the stirrup, and then she swung into the saddle with a great flurry of petticoats and skirts. She was seemingly oblivious to how her clothes and underclothes rode up around her hips. But the sight of it, even in his condition, gave Longarm an erection. He remembered how warm and soft and wet she had been.

He swung into his saddle, flinching as he did. He had

146

pulled Marianne's stirrups up, but they still seemed a little too long. He was about to say that he would get down and take them up for her, but she shook her head. "These will be just fine," she said. "I don't really pay much attention to the stirrups. I learned to ride bareback. Sitting in this saddle will be as easy as pie."

Longarm said, "Now, you know what you're doing?"

"I think so."

"This is going to be one hell of a ride over some rough country. You said that mining camp was three miles away, or it could be ten or it could be twelve or it could be fifteen. It's very easy to lose your bearings in the desert."

She shrugged. "Hadn't we better get going?"

Marianne was completely right. The moon was up full now. For a while, they would be hidden from the Hunsackers as they trailed north. The Hunsackers camp was directly south, and the rocks and eruptions would conceal him and Marianne for a time. He didn't know how long it would be before the Hunsackers caught their trail. He had no earthly idea. He had loaded his horse and Marianne's horse with two rifles and a shotgun, and he had his six-gun at hand. He could get off twenty shots in all, including the two shotgun barrels.

He nudged his bay forward. "Well, let's give it a try," he said. As his horse moved, he took the roan on lead, starting for the north gate. Marianne pulled up beside him, both of them walking their horses across the rocks on the floor of the rock outcropping. The place had served its purpose. It had given him a chance to reduce the Hunsacker gang and dim their eagerness. Maybe it had hurt them so bad they'd go to ground and lick their wounds for a while.

But he really didn't think so. He was almost certain they

147

would be hot on his trail when they realized he and Marianne were gone. He didn't know if he had time enough to clean up his wound. If he didn't, he would be in bad shape before they reached help. He could already feel himself getting lighter in the head.

They trailed out through the northern entrance. It seemed the great expanse of desert lit up in front of them with the big full moon shining down.

Longarm said to Marianne, "Well, good luck to both of us."

She said grimly, "I think you're the one that needs it."

Chapter 9

For the first ten minutes, neither of them spoke. The only sounds around the desert were the soft shuffle of their horses' hooves and the creaking of their saddles. Longarm kept them pointed due north to keep the rock outcropping between himself and the Hunsackers. After he had gone about three quarters of a mile, he pulled up his horse. Beside him, Marianne did the same. He turned as best as he could in the saddle with his side paining him as bad as it was. He looked back. The Hunsacker camp was still obscured by the rock formations, but he could faintly hear the sound of someone screaming riding on the desert wind.

Marianne said dryly, "That would be Verlene telling the Hunsackers that she is waiting to be fetched back to their camp."

Longarm said, "That ain't all she's telling them. We'd better get on the move."

He picked up the pace ever so slightly. It wouldn't do to wear the horses out. On foot, they would very likely be targets out in the middle of nowhere. He turned to Marianne as they made their slow way across the desert. "How's the compass working in your head?" he said. "Do you have any better idea where that mining camp is?"

She gestured to her left. "The best I can remember, it's over that way. But . . . I can't be sure."

"You were pretty specific when you were talking about it. Do you know if it's three miles, five miles, or seven miles?"

Marianne shook her head slowly, her blond hair catching the glow of the moon. "I don't know. I didn't realize it would be necessary for me to remember a thing like that. I didn't know we were coming here to get in a war."

Longarm said, "It ain't a war, Marianne. It's a law officer trying to bring criminals to justice. If you'd been one of their victims, you might not think so kindly of them."

She shrugged. "Well, I have no reason to think otherwise. I've never been their victim. They've paid me well for my services. They've been drunk and disorderly, but then so are cowboys who work on ranches."

They rode on in silence. In time, Longarm said, "You know, I guess I ought to be surprised with you, but I ain't. You said you were going to do this and I doubted you then. I didn't see any reason for you to face the hard cold facts of the matter, but you did." He looked around at the young woman riding to his right. "You're better than you think you are."

She said, "I don't look down my nose at myself, Marshal Long. That's *your* doing. Do you think I'm not capable of being kind because I'm a whore?"

Longarm shook his head. "Being a whore has nothing to do with it. Frankly, I don't think you *are* one. In your heart, that is. What I'm talking about is going up to the Hunsackers' camp under the pretense of getting married."

"How do you know we weren't?"

Longarm smiled. "Because you've come with me, that's why. For my money, I think you got talked into doing something you didn't want to do. The closer you got to it, the more you wanted out. I think I'm your chance. What do you say to that?"

In the moonlight, he almost saw her flush slightly. He supposed it was just his imagination. She said, "Don't flatter yourself. I don't need your chance. I'm coming along with you because I want to. Let it be that."

Longarm laughed softly. "Just as you say."

A little further along, she said, glancing at the sky, "What time do you suppose it is?"

Longarm looked at the rising moon. "Oh, I reckon it's a little after midnight. I could get out my watch, but it's a little too dark to see. Thank heavens for that. We're getting a few clouds helping us."

"How much time before you think they find out you're gone?"

"I don't think that Verlene's screaming is going to fetch them. I'd think they'd be a mite cautious about riding up toward those rocks. For all they know, I might have gotten Verlene, either through threat or persuasion or purchase, to set up a squall to draw them in. There's not but about four or five of them left as I counted. If they got within a hundred yards of the rocks with the moon bright, I could get them all. So, I think they'll be cautious about tonight."

He looked over at her. "In a way, I'm kind of betting my life on it. We need to get enough distance between us and them for me to open this wound up and get some of this corruption out of my side. I'm hoping they don't get hot behind us.''

She shrugged again. ''I think you can count on the fact that Verlene won't do anything but scream.''

''You don't think she'll try walking across that desert to their camp?''

''Not at night. Not as afraid as she is of the outdoors.''

Longarm nodded his head at her. ''You sit a horse like you're used to being outdoors.''

Marianne shrugged again. ''I grew up in Wyoming. There you did what you had to do in order to get by. If you couldn't ride a horse, you'd freeze walking.''

Longarm said, ''Yeah, that's pretty country but it can be deadly. I sure hope you are right about Verlene. If she'll sit right where she is, maybe I've got time to get to that mining camp.''

Marianne looked at him. ''If we can find it. Can't we go any faster?''

Longarm shook his head. ''I don't know how far we've got to go, so I don't want to use these horses too hard. If it comes to it, we might have to run a spell, so I need them ready.'' He was glad for the coolness of the night because he could feel the fever working through his body. He knew he was getting sicker.

They rode on and on, holding a northerly course at first, and then veering off to the left, toward the west. Marianne had no sense of where the mining camp was located. She grew vaguer and vaguer in her suggestions. Finally, Longarm struck a route a few points to the left of the North Star. They plowed on through the small hours heading toward dawn, hoping desperately that they could find someplace before the Hunsackers arrived.

Time after time, turning in his saddle, Longarm looked back, but the horizon stayed clear. He guessed Marianne was right that Verlene couldn't draw the Hunsackers with her screams and that she was too afraid of the desert at night to make her own way to their camp. He knew he and Marianne would leave a clear trail on the desert floor. The sandy dirt was too loose and soft to hide their fresh tracks, which would be visible even to the untrained eye the next morning.

Once, Marianne rode up next to him and put her left hand out to his face. She said with concern in her voice, "Marshal Long, we've got to find someplace quick to do something about you. If we don't, the Hunsackers will have already killed you."

Longarm felt his face. He was sweating, even as the air grew cooler. He said, "Yeah, I know, but we can't just stop here in the middle of nothing. Hell, if we could just find an old river bottom or a ravine or a gully or a little hill. Anything. But I don't see anything. Just all this damned desert. They would see us from two miles off, sure as hell, if we pulled up. We're going to have to build a fire, and they'll damned sure see that."

"We've got to do something soon," she said.

"I know."

It was Marianne who spotted the structure first. An hour or so after she had touched his face, she said, "What's that?" Her words came sharp in the cold air.

Longarm said, "What? I don't see...." His eyes scanned the horizon. He thought maybe she was seeing the first signs of daylight. He knew it shouldn't be long before dawn. The moon had been down for a good hour or so. "What are you talking about?"

She stopped her horse and pointed to the left of their line of march. In the distance, he could see the low run of foothills that stretched into the mountains. The Sierra Madres, he knew they were called.

Longarm stopped his horse also, and narrowed his eyes, but everything faded into the rounded hills that were still a good way off. He said, "I don't see anything."

Marianne poked an insistant finger out. "There to the left of that rounded hill."

He peered hard in the darkness. Sure enough, he saw a sharp corner that didn't belong to the roundness of the hill. He said, "Just there? Just yonder?"

She nodded. "Yes, it looks like a cabin."

"Well, your eyes are sharper than mine, which ain't most often the case. Let's head for it."

They urged their horses forward, and aimed a little west by northwest. As they rode, he asked her if she thought it was part of the mining camp. She shook her head. "I don't know. All I can see is just the one cabin. The mining camp has five or six, and then there was a two-story frame house where we stayed. They brought the lumber in from Reno."

Now he could see the dim outline of what she had seen earlier. It was indeed the framework of a lone cabin with nothing else around it. It appeared to be about two miles away, but then, distances were so deceptive in the desert. He said, "Well, let's get on up to it. If it's what I think it is, I don't want to be riding after dawn, and I don't reckon that's more than an hour away."

In fifteen minutes, they were approaching the cabin, and even in the darkness, Longarm could tell it wasn't much. It was built of native rock with a tin roof. It never pretended to be more than it was—a one-room miner's cabin. As they neared, Longarm could see that it was on a downslope, facing down into the foothills. By then, they were close enough that they could see a dry streambed in front of the cabin.

The yard of the place told its own story.

Long years past, some optimistic miner had built the cabin on the banks of a creek that had been flowing at that time. He'd had the water to wash his gold, but the falling-down roof of the place attested to the fact that the water hadn't lasted and neither had the miner. With the loss of the water, either through drought or the lack of snow in the mountains to make its way down to form the creek, the miner hadn't been able to water himself or his stock or his gold, and had had to pull up stakes.

But the lone cabin would do for Longarm's purposes. It would give him cover while they tended to his wound. If the Hunsackers came up on him, either while he and Marianne were draining out the corruption or while he was resting up from the operation, the outlaws would pay a dear price if they tried to approach.

Longarm led them straight to the front of the cabin. He dismounted, and then gave Marianne his shoulder as an aid as she came down from the high saddle to the ground. The cabin was in worse repair than it had seemed from a distance. Longarm reckoned that it had been falling apart for some ten years or so, not that that really mattered. If the water had stayed in the streambed, there would have been a lot of other cabins stretched out along its length.

He led the three horses through the narrow door, one at a time, into the cabin. He guessed it to be not much bigger than sixteen feet by sixteen, but he didn't want to leave the horses outside. With his strength draining out of him, he still took the time to uncinch the two saddles and take the bits out of their mouths. The horses seemed in pretty good shape. Fortunately, the walls of the cabin were high enough that they would be protected from gunfire. There were two windows, one at the back and one to the west. The door opened from the north. Longarm said, "Well, I reckon we can set up housekeeping here. What do we have for vital goods besides a canteen of water?"

Marianne shrugged. "I think there may be a can of tomatoes and a can of peaches and maybe a little piece of cheese. Other than that, I guess we're going to have to make do with sand and cactus."

Longarm said, "How are we planning on going about this?" He put his hand to his side.

Marianne said, "We're going to need a fire. I'll go and collect some wood."

"You ain't scared of the desert at night?"

She shook her head. "Anybody that's ever lived in this kind of country knows that snakes and varmints go to ground in the cold of the morning. They don't come out until the sun does."

She disappeared out the door, and Longarm sat down to wait. The horses were huddled over in a far corner, looking at him curiously. The cabin was dark, but Longarm's eyes had adjusted well enough so that he could see. It wasn't but a few moments until Marianne was back with a small bundle of dried mesquite limbs and twigs and branches off of some small greasewood bushes. They were dry, and they would burn hot and without smoke. Not, he guessed, that the Hunsackers were going to have any trouble finding where he had gone to.

Marianne put her load down, expertly built the twigs into

a pile, and added branches. Longarm struck a match, and the tinder caught almost instantly. In a matter of a few minutes, they had a bright blaze going. Marianne added bigger sticks to the fire until it spread a circle of warmth that was welcome in the cold of the coming morning.

Marianne looked at him. "I reckon you'd better get your knife out," she said.

Longarm nodded. He wasn't particularly looking forward to the proceedings, but he didn't see any way around them. He knew he was sick. He was hurting, and he knew he wasn't going to get better until certain steps were taken. Marianne went over to the saddlebags and came back with the small skillet that Longarm carried. She filled it with water and set it against the coals that were building up as the wood burned down. Then she took the jackknife that Longarm had handed her, opened the blade, and washed it in the water until she deemed it clean. She left it in the water with the handle away from the fire while the edge of the water began to tremble slightly as it heated on the coals.

She said, "The knife seems sharp enough."

Longarm was unbuttoning his shirt. He didn't have to be told what to do. He said, "I'd as soon carry an empty gun as a dull knife. It would make about as much sense." He finished stripping off his shirt, and carefully laid it on the dirt floor of the cabin beside the fire.

Before he knelt down, he untied the knot in the bandage that Marianne had put on the day before. He unwound it and dropped it on the floor. The two pads covering the front part of the wound and the back part didn't fall off. He knew they were dried to his skin by the blood. He reached for a corner of the bandage in the front, and Marianne stayed his hand. She said, "You better wait and let me work that loose. I don't want it tearing off the scab any more than it has to. I'll moisten it with some water when it gets to boiling.''

Longarm slumped down next to the fire in a position where he could lay on his right side, exposing his left side to Marianne. "You're the boss," he said.

"How are you feeling?"

Longarm shook his head slightly from side to side. "I've been better, but then I've also been shot before. Generally, however, I've taken better care of myself."

She said, "I don't think it's gone too far." She reached under her skirt and tore loose another piece of petticoat. She soaked it in the now-bubbling water in the skillet, took it out, and then let it cool a little. She circled the fire before she knelt down beside Longarm. She held the moist piece of cloth against the back bandage, gradually and gently pulling at the edge. He felt it come loose. She cast the used bandage away in the corner, and then began on the bandage in the front. It hurt a little more, and Longarm was surprised. He said, "Hell, I'd have thought that big one in the back was worse off."

She said, "No, it made a bigger hole coming out. It ain't quite healed up. It looks like most of the infection is in the front."

"That's halfway good to hear."

She said, "That doesn't mean that I don't have to reopen the back."

"I thought that's what you were going to say."

She reached under her clothes and pulled off the slip she had been ripping. In spite of himself, Longarm stirred at the sight of her long bare golden legs flashing in the firelight. She took the petticoat and ripped it into long strips,

158

then put them, one by one, into the boiling water.

Longarm said, "Ain't we nearly there?"

She said, "Just about."

"Well, in my saddlebag, there's a bottle of whiskey. I'd appreciate it if you would fetch it for me."

She got up, went over to his horse, and rummaged around for a moment, and then came back with the bottle, which was still half full. She uncorked it and handed it to him. He looked at her and said, "You might as well throw that cork away. I don't reckon to have much use for it for the next couple of hours."

She silently pitched the cork out the front door, and knelt down beside him again and then took the knife by the handle. She said, "I'm going to heat this knife in the fire because I'm hoping to sear that wound when I open it up so that it won't get reinfected."

Longarm was having a long, hard pull on the bottle. He said, "Yeah, I was afraid you'd know about that. That's what you're supposed to do. I guess you also know about sticking tents in the wound."

In the dim light, he could see her nod. "Yeah," she said. "Those pieces of bandages that I've got cooking, when they get to boiling, I'll take that knife and set it in the coals and use the bandages. I'm going to have to get it hot, Marshal. You ain't going to jump or anything, are you? It'll just make it worse."

"I'll hold as steady as I can," Longarm said. "Wish I had saved that cork now."

"What for?"

"Give me something to bite on."

He could see her take the knife out of the skillet of boiling water and hold it just over the hot coals. He could see the blade tint red. He had no illusions about what was coming.

She said, "We'll do the front first. It'll be the worst, Marshal. I know it's going to hurt."

"Hell, you might as well call me Longarm. That's my nickname."

"Yeah, I've heard that. I didn't know if you liked to be called that by anyone other than your friends."

He said, "Well, what do you reckon we are now? You taking advantage of me in my sleep, you running off with me, and now you're fixing to stick something in me just like I stuck something in you. Although I believe yours is going to be a little hotter. I reckon that makes us pretty close."

She smiled at him when she picked up the handle of the knife. "I'm going to be quick now." Out of the corner of his eye, he saw her make a motion.

It seemed he could smell the burning flesh before the pain really jolted him. When the hurt got to him, it arrived full-blown, like a Texas tornado. It was all he could do to snuff a groan.

She said, "My God. You wouldn't believe what's coming out of here, Longarm. I'm surprised you are still alive."

Through clenched teeth, he said, "I'm so glad to hear that."

"I've got to wash this knife off and then get it hot again for the back."

Longarm said, "I can't wait." It was all he could do to strangle down a scream.

He waited for a second thrust. It was only just a little easier than the front. Then it was over.

She said, "It wasn't built up in the back like it was in

160

the front. Hopefully it will drain real good. I'm going to get those tents ready so we don't have to do this again.''

Longarm had laid his head down on his arm. He felt too weak to be weary, and he didn't try to answer. Yet at the same time, he could almost feel himself getting better, as if the fever was draining out of his body along with the blood and the infection. He still didn't try to answer. He just lay quietly as he felt her working over him. He felt her poking the long strips that were soaking wet and still hot from the boiling water in both sides of his body. Then he felt her put a pad around his side that covered both of the wounds.

Marianne said, ''You look all white-faced. I'm not going to ask you to raise up so I can get this bandage around you. I think if you'll lay there for a while, you'll be best off.''

Longarm said, ''Thanks. Hand me that bottle, will you?''

She moved and put it in his hand. It had only been some six inches away, but he hadn't been able to see it. He couldn't quite lift it, so she raised it to his lips for him. He was able to raise his head enough to pull down several swallows. Then he said, ''Ahhh . . .'' and laid his head back down.

''You still with me? You gonna make it?''

He said, ''Oh, yeah. I'll be making it. You've done a good job. I'm much obliged to you.''

She said, ''I've done things I've enjoyed more, I've got to say that. That wound was a mess. I think that bullet could have splintered when it went into you. It's kind of a funny-looking entrance wound, and the back is really a mess.''

Longarm said faintly, ''That's just what I need. Another good scar.''

He could feel her move the bandage pads in the front

and back. She said, "I can see that some of the redness is going away, but they are still draining. I am going to let them drain a little while longer before I bandage you up."

He worked his way up to his elbow and had another pull of the whiskey. "I reckon as long as the whiskey holds out, I can stand it," he said. "But I've got to tell you, little girl, I can already feel that poison draining out of me. I'm not ready to run a footrace with an Indian, but I'm already feeling stronger."

She said, "I don't think you should get too spry just yet. Wait."

He looked around at her, kneeling by his side, studying his wounds. Her face was very beautiful in the firelight. He said, "Marianne, we can't wait too long. We're here in the desert with no water and no food for these horses. You and I can last three or four days without water. We've got water for us, but these horses can't last. They haven't got any water. We've got to get to someplace where there is help. I've got to go on whether I'm sick or not."

She said, "Just let it drain for a few more minutes."

He laid his head back down and stared into the fire as she built up the flames. The coals were still very apparent in the heavy morning. The air seemed to carry some moisture, even though it probably hadn't rained in this country in five years. Sometimes it rained in the mountains, and it nearly always snowed in the mountains. When the snow melted in the spring and summer, it ran down into little creeks that gave prospectors hope that it was a livable land. But it was a dangerous, treacherous land. The water you found today might not be there tomorrow.

It felt very comfortable lying on his side, feeling himself get better, but he was still so tired and sleepy.

He let his eyes blink a few times, and then closed them. His mind seemed far away. It felt pleasant and warm by the fire, and somehow secure within the rock walls of the broken-down cabin. It seemed only a moment later when he heard Marianne say, "I believe sunrise has come."

Relunctantly, he fluttered his eyes open. He could tell at a glance that the light in the cabin had taken on a different texture. It was no longer quilted with black. It was now much lighter, starting to show traces of sunlight.

He said, "Oh, hell. I could have wished for it to have stayed dark a little longer. At least long enough to where they couldn't track our sign before noon."

Marianne said, "You had better sit up and let me bandage those pads on your wounds. I've got the long strips I can wind around you. It needs some pressure to keep you from bleeding overmuch. I reckon you've lost all the blood you need to lose."

He put his shirt back on, but he kept it hiked up high on his chest. Now, when he sat up, he had to keep it held up as she wound the bandage around his midriff. Surprisingly, there was very little pain. He said, "You'd think a body would hurt after having a red-hot knife stuck in it a couple of places."

She tied off the knot and looked up at him and smiled. "That was about a half bottle of whiskey ago," She said. "I wouldn't think you'd be feeling anything by now."

"Normally, I drink that much before breakfast," he said. "But since we ain't going to have any breakfast, I guess it's just as well I drank it."

She got up and crossed to where the skillet sat. The canteen was right beside it. She brought it back to him and made him drink. "You need to keep plenty of water in your system," she said. "They say it's good for a body."

He drank, forcing some of the water down, not all that thirsty. When he was finished, he handed her the canteen and said, "The same goes for you."

As she drank, he admired her and her slim neck and the way her breast rose against the material of her thin muslin frock. It caused a faint stirring in his loins. It seemed silly even to him. Here he was with some bad outlaws tracking him, wounded and sick, with no food, in the middle of the desert, and he was thinking about lusting for her flesh. That took some kind of optimism, he figured.

He watched her thoughtfully until she had finished drinking. She lowered the canteen and then put the top back on it.

He said, "You know, Marianne, you're quite a lady."

She gave a short laugh. "I haven't been called that very often."

"It ain't what you do for a living that makes you a lady or not a lady. It's the way you conduct yourself in the general business of living. To me, you're a grand lady."

She gave him an amused look. "I believe that's the first compliment I ever had from a lawman."

"Well, if I'm around, it won't be the last."

She cocked her head to one side and studied him. "You know, I've heard about you," she said. "I knew your nickname was Longarm. You're supposed to be this dangerous, never-give-up, chase-them-to-the-end-of-the-earth federal marshal. And yet, you don't seem quite as hard and tough as I expected you to be."

He chuckled slightly. "I don't reckon I look like much right now. I think I've lost about ten pounds in the last few days. I feel a little drawn."

She said, "You also haven't had any sleep. Why don't you catch a little nap? I'll watch carefully."

He looked at her closely, narrowing his eyes. "I recollect that it wasn't too long ago that you more or less helped me to want to sleep."

To his surprise, her cheeks reddened in a blush. She glanced down at her hands. "I wish you wouldn't remind me of that. I'd like to say that Verlene talked me into doing that, but to tell you the truth, it was my idea." She looked up at him. "And I didn't really do it to make you sleep."

He half smiled and said, "I didn't think you did."

She gave him a stern look. "Well, don't be thinking about it. A body can be curious, that's all. Now, why don't you lay your head down and I'll call you in an hour."

Longarm said, "All right," and then laid his head gratefully on his arm. His body felt as if it had been ridden a long, long way without food or rest. He closed his eyes. He supposed sleep overcame him instantly.

How long he slept, he wasn't sure of at first. Words seem to come filtering through his consciousness. At first, the words didn't make any sense. Then gradually as his mind came awake, he heard them clearly. It was Marianne. She said, "Longarm! Wake up! They're coming! Longarm! Longarm!"

He willed his eyes to open. The first thing he was aware of was the brilliant light, and the second was how warm it was in the cabin. Dawn had long since passed. He heard Marianne call to him again, and he slowly and painfully worked himself up to a sitting position. She was in the back of the cabin, peering around the corner of the window. He said, still half asleep, "What is it?"

Marianne said, "They're coming, Longarm. You'd better

get over here if you can and see what you think.''

Longarm didn't dare stand up. He was fearful that as faint and weak as he was, he might fall over, so on hands and knees, he crawled over the base of the small window and raised himself up cautiously until he could see over the ledge.

He could see a trail of black dots heading directly toward them. It took a moment to separate them, but he could tell the first dots were four horsemen with a bigger dot behind them. The other dot was probably the wagon with extra horses being towed along. He turned and sat back down, propping his back against the wall. Marianne looked at him. ''It's them, isn't it?'' she said.

''I don't reckon it'd be anybody else.''

She was a long time in asking the question, but it came with no less impact. She said, ''What are you going to do?''

Chapter 10

He was equally as long in answering. Finally, he said, "I don't know."

She looked out the window again, just peering around the edge. "You better think of something quick," she said. "I don't reckon they're more than two miles off."

Longarm nodded. "That'd be about right, and at the rate they're coming, they'll be here in less than an hour."

Marianne moved away from the window, walked across the cabin to the door, and looked through it to the foothills in the distance. She said, "What about those mountains? Can't we hide in them?"

Longarm gave a small chuckle. "We? Have you joined up?"

She gave him an angry look. "Dammit, I didn't help you to stay alive just to see you shot down. Don't be sarcastic with me. I'll be sarcastic back if you start it with me."

Longarm didn't bother to apologize. He said, shaking his head, "No, we wouldn't make it to the foothills, and it wouldn't be a good place to hide. It would take me too long to get the horses ready, and as weak as I am, I'm not sure I could make it. My best chance is to hope they get discouraged in trying to take me and give up.''

She said, ''But you can't hold out here very long. All we have is some water.''

He looked at her across the cabin. He said softly, ''Marianne, I don't want you staying here with me. There's going to be lead flying around in here. You go to them. You've done enough for me as it is. I'm very much obliged to you.''

She said firmly, ''I'm not leaving you. Get that straight.''

''But if you got to them, they won't have any reason to press home the battle against me. It could be costly rushing this place, and I can hold out for three or four days with nothing but water.''

Marianne said, ''They are going to know that you are wounded.''

''How are they going to know that?''

She said, ''Because there was blood in too many places in that rock fort. You dripped blood in both of the caves.''

It made him think for a moment. ''Well, so what? How does that change anything?''

''It means that they'll know that you are weak and wounded and that you can't hold out very long. They'll wait one more day and then one more. That'll be the end of you. If I stay in here, they can't shoot in the cabin.''

''Hell, Marianne. I don't want you taking that chance. You're dealing with people that you don't really understand. The Hunsackers ain't very nice folks. If they don't got no further use for you, they don't really care what happens to you. I'm trying to tell you that if they're angry enough at me, they wouldn't care if you got hit by a stray bullet or not. You've got to trust me on this. I've known the Hunsackers and their kind for a lot of years. The milk of human kindness has dried up in their udders a long time ago.''

She looked across the cabin. ''Are you saying that you want me to go out with people like that? You want me to go and join them?''

Her eyes made him feel uncomfortable. He said, ''I think it would be a hell of a lot safer.''

She said, ''Maybe I don't think that way. Maybe I don't want to be around people like the Hunsackers.''

Longarm pursed his lips. ''Well, I'm not going to shove you out the door, but I will tell you that it's liable to get a little fierce in here. There ain't too many places to hide in this square room, and we don't have enough tin on the roof to hold off rain, much less lead.''

She said, ''Then you'd better think of something because I'm not going out.''

Longarm turned cautiously and applied his left eye to the corner of the window. The dots were no longer dots. They had turned into horsemen and a wagon being pulled by a team trailing several horses. Longarm could see big barrels of water sitting in the bed of the wagon.

It looked to him as if there were two women on the seat of the wagon. He guessed it would be Verlene and Minnie Sewell. He reckoned Minnie was driving the team. That would leave the men free to attack him from all directions.

Even as he watched, the group began veering off to the west. They weren't going to come within range of his rifle. If he was any judge of Hunsacker and his habits and his cowardly ways, the four men left would simply surround the cabin at a distance and wait for Longarm to try to make a break for it. He doubted there would be much conversation.

He turned back into the room. Marianne had crossed back over to the window, and was standing on the other side. She said, "Well?"

Longarm shook his head. "I don't know. I don't see any way to draw them close enough to do any good. They've brought the wagon, and that means that they're going to have plenty of provisions for both themselves and their horses. Mainly they'll have water for their horses. That's the one thing we ain't got. Beats the hell out of me what to do."

She said, "Maybe I can do something."

Longarm gave her a hard look. "Just hold up there, missy. I don't want you looking brave. I got brave when I run into that hornet's nest back there in Lodestar. I should have been much better prepared, but I was in a hurry to get home. Now it looks like I'm going to be delayed much longer than I thought."

He glanced quickly around the corner of the window, and then came back to her side of the room. The sun was now high enough so that the rays were coming through the ruined roof. It wouldn't be long before it was hot enough to suit anyone. Longarm said, "There's a fellow back in Denver that would get a big kick out of this. A chief marshal by the name of Billy Vail. He's always going on as to how I have it so easy. Well, I wish he could see the fix I've gotten myself into now. Maybe he wouldn't be so quick to tell me that I need to back up to the pay window."

Marianne said as she looked around the edge, "They're closer. They're going further around to the west."

170

Longarm nodded. "They want to stay out of rifle shot." He peered around the window and saw the caravan bearing off to the left. They were less than a half mile away.

Longarm said, "There's nothing we can do now but wait."

Wait, he thought, until they have us good and surrounded, and then wait as they draw the noose tighter as the water runs out. Just then, one of his horses smelled the Hunsackers' stock and whined loudly. The noise was loud in the small cabin, and both Longarm and Marianne jumped.

Marianne said, "Dammit, they'll hear that."

Longarm shrugged. "It doesn't make a damn. They know we are in here. The signs run straight to this cabin. As soon as they circle, they're going to know we didn't go on, so the horse letting out a holler doesn't make any difference." He slumped down on the floor again, trying to think of something. His weapons were so few—a derringer, two six-guns, and two rifles. The rifles were practically useless since the Hunsackers would never come within range. No they'd just cast their net around the cabin and pull it in.

After a few more moments, he looked around the window ledge. He was surprised to see that the caravan was going on toward the north. He had expected for certain that they would deploy behind him to the east, but they were staying together. He motioned for Marianne to go to the door and see what she could see.

Longarm watched as she went low on the floor and peeked around the corner of the door at the lowest level she could get her face to. She moved slowly so that her movement would not attract attention. She watched for a full five minutes. Finally, she pulled back and raised up and said, "They're gone straight to the north of us and pulled up. It looks to be Verlene and Mrs. Sewell, and the best that I can tell, it's Shank and LeeRoy and the old man. I don't recognize the fourth person. It could be Joe."

Longarm said, "I was hoping that Shank was dead. You say they are all there?"

She nodded. "Yes."

He was much surprised. They apparently did not intend to surround him, at least not yet. As painful as it was to do, he had to take a look. He sidled around the far wall so he was out of sight through the open door, then got in behind Marianne, feeling the softness of her flesh as she leaned back into him, and took a quick look around the door frame. There was no mistake. They had parked the wagon about six hundred yards away and unhitched the team. The rest of the horses were being watered. One man was doing the job, and Longarm recognized J.J. and LeeRoy and Shank as they stood, staring at the cabin.

After a moment, the old man walked forward, putting his hands to his mouth, cupping them. He yelled out, his words carrying easily through the thin air, "Longarm, we be knowin' you're in there. Ain't no way for you to get away. You let that girl come on out and we'll give you your life. That's the best bargain you're ever going to get."

Longarm leaned away from the door, resting his back against the cabin wall. Marianne followed him. She looked up in his face. "What does it mean?" she said.

Longarm half smiled. "It means that I'm damned if I do and I'm damned if I don't."

Marianne said, "If I were to go to them, they'd leave you alone. Do you believe that?"

Longarm smiled again. "Do you believe it? What do you think?"

She said, after a moment's thought, "No, your reputation is that you never quit, that you would always be chasing them. They couldn't afford to let you live. No, I don't believe them."

"But Verlene and Mrs. Sewell are there. Wouldn't you feel better with them?"

She gave him an odd look. "You still don't really understand me, do you?"

He looked down at the dusty floor. "Marianne, we haven't exactly known each other that long. Sometimes I don't even know myself."

The voice of J.J. Hunsacker came floating through the hot air to them. "Longarm, we ain't going to give you until the cows come home to make up your mind. We could put a hail of bullets right through that open door and fix your wagon pretty good. We could get enough lead bouncing around in there that would put more holes in you than a sieve. If you're as smart as you think you are, you'd turn that girl loose and save your life."

Marianne said, looking up at him again, "There's nothing really to do."

Longarm shook his head. "All I'll do is push you out that door."

Marianne said, "You go lay down there where you were when I dressed your wounds on your bedroll."

He gave her a questioning look. "Whatever for?"

She was studying his face, looking into his eyes. "Are you a good shot?"

He frowned, wrinkling his brow. "I don't know what you mean by a good shot. I reckon I'm a fair shot, yes."

"No, I mean with a handgun in close quarters. Is your hand steady and your nerves good?"

He wrinkled his brow even more. "I don't know what you are talking about, Marianne. But yes, I reckon I'm a pretty good shot at close quarters. I wouldn't be alive otherwise. In fact, I wouldn't be alive in any kind of quarters other than being a damn good shot."

She said, "That's what I thought."

"So? What does all this mean?"

"You go lay down on your bedroll and have your guns real handy."

"What are you going to do?"

"I'm going to get them up here in range for you."

Longarm said, "Like hell you are! Marianne, I don't know what you're up to, but . . ."

He got no further. She had suddenly stepped into the opening of the door and called in a loud voice, "J.J.! LeeRoy! Come here!"

Longarm moved swiftly to lay on his bedroll. It was placed at an angle to the door so that anyone coming through it would have to look to their left to see him.

The horses were jammed against the wall. He said, "What in the hell are you doing, Marianne? You're going to get yourself hurt."

She said, without turning her head, "You be sure you can shoot straight. Is your gun loaded?"

"I told you, I don't carry dull knives or unloaded guns."

Marianne called out again. "LeeRoy, he's wounded and he's about to die. Come up. He might be able to shoot me if I try and make a run for it, but he's very weak. He can't even sit up. Hurry!"

174

From behind her, Longarm said, "Have you ever considered going on the stage, Marianne?"

"You know," she said, "this may not be right. I don't like this, Longarm. You're going to make too good of a target. Why don't you get up and get out the back window. There's nobody out there to see you."

Seeing the rightness of it, he said, "I think you're on the right path, but I ain't sure I can get out the window."

She said urgently, "You've got to. They're starting this way."

"All of them?"

"Yes, except for the women. The four men are coming."

Longarm said, "I'm trying. I'm up on all fours. I can't take my rifle. That window ledge looks about six feet high. My God, I can't believe how weak I am." Holding his hand to his side, he hobbled over to the window, and painfully eased one leg over the rock ledge. "What are they doing now?"

"They are still coming. No, wait! One is staying behind. I think it's Joe."

Longarm said, "Are you sure Joe is with them?"

Marianne said, "It might not be, but LeeRoy and Shank and J.J. are coming on."

Longarm said, "I'm about out this window and I've only got six slugs in this gun. What are you going to do when they walk through that door and don't see nobody?"

"That's your job. I'm just supposed to get them in here."

"Why don't you get some saddle blankets off those horses, and my saddlebags and the canteen and anything else that you can think of, and put them in my bedroll. Maybe they will think that it's me under there."

175

She didn't wait to answer. She commenced to gather up what she could under the bedroll, putting his saddle up at the top, spreading a blanket over it so that it looked like he was using the saddle for a pillow. It was not very deceiving, but then it did not have to deceive very long. Through the window, Longarm said, "How far off are they?"

Marianne stepped to the door and looked around. "About a hundred yards. No, now they've stopped."

Longarm said, "Are they armed?"

"Yes, but they don't have their guns in their hands. Well, Mr. Hunsacker is carrying a rifle, but he's just got it loose in his hand."

"Are they still coming?"

Marianne said, "No, they've stopped again. Mr. Hunsacker is yelling something."

They both listened. Hunsacker shouted, "Longarm, if you be in there, now's the time to get out. We're liable to come in there with gunplay and you're going to be mighty sorry."

Unbidden, Marianne stepped back into the door. She called out, "Mr. Hunsacker, he may be dead. I'm scared to get close to him. There's blood all over the floor and all over his blanket."

At the window, Longarm heard J.J. Hunsacker's voice clearly. "Well, I don't wish him no harm." Then the old man chuckled. "Other than a long, slow, painful death out here amongst these rattlesnakes and big spiders. Why don't you come on, girl?"

She said, "I'll get my stuff, but I need somebody to help me carry it out and help me with the horses."

Hunsacker said, "Well, that varmint of a marshal better

not give us no trouble or he's going to wish he'd never been born.''

Outside the window, Longarm slowly pulled the hammer back on his revolver. With his eye at the bottom of the window, he could see out through the front door. He saw a pair of legs, then a half body, and then the bodies of the three men suddenly appear, walking toward the cabin. In another minute, he saw the faces of the old man and LeeRoy and Shank. Marianne had moved to the right of the door. Longarm waited. It would be another ten seconds. He steeled his hand, as weak as it was. He was going to give them a chance to surrender if that was what they chose.

The three men stood just inside the cabin, looking around. The old man had a carbine rifle that hung loosely in his hands. At his side, LeeRoy and Shank were both holding pistols down by their sides. They looked around. LeeRoy said, ''Well, hell. There ain't nobody in here!'' He glanced over at Marianne. ''There ain't nobody in here, woman. Where is that sonofabitch?''

That instant, Longarm suddenly stood up outside the window. He said, ''Here's that sonofabitch, right here, right now!''

Their heads swiveled around toward him, turning away from Marianne. J.J. Hunsacker said, ''Why, Longarm! You low-down, sneaky sonofabitch! You got a woman to do your lying for you?''

Longarm crouched so that he made as small a target as possible. ''Throw down your guns, right now!'' he said.

J.J. looked around at Marianne. He motioned his rifle toward her.

Longarm said, ''Drop that weapon, J.J. Hunsacker, or I'll take you quick and sudden!''

LeeRoy and Shank raised their revolvers and fired, the shots coming almost together, the noise making a loud booming racket in the stone cabin. Longarm felt his face sting as the bullets hit the rock around the window opening, spraying him with splinters. In almost the same heartbeat, he had fired, taking Shank on the left with a bullet right in the chest. The slug knocked the young man backwards. He saw the man's gun slipping out of his lifeless fingers.

Without pause, Longarm was already aiming at LeeRoy, who was trying to get off a second shot. Longarm's revolver roared toward the bandit. He had tried for a throat shot, but the bullet went high and hit LeeRoy just above his mouth, blowing his nose back into his head. The shot sent him toppling backwards, almost as if the slug had struck bone.

But Longarm had no time to observe the results of his shot. Even as LeeRoy was falling to the cabin floor, Longarm was swinging on the old man, centering the sight of his revolver on J.J.'s chest.

The old man had his rifle almost to his shoulders, pointing directly at Longarm in the window.

Longarm said, "Drop it, J.J.! Put that rifle down or I'll put a hole right through you!"

For an instant, Longarm wasn't certain whether the old man was going to stop or would have to be shot. The man's hand slowed, and the butt of the rifle never reached his shoulder. Instead, he slowly lowered the weapon until the carbine was hanging by his side.

Longarm said, "Drop it all the way, old man!"

J.J. Hunsacker let go of his carbine. It clattered to the dust floor of the cabin. He stared at Longarm with hate in his face and his eyes and his voice. He said, "You dirty sonofabitch. What are you doing out there? You're supposed to be in here, bad wounded or dead.''

Longarm said, "I'm out here because that's just where I am. Now, get your hands up."

The old man's voice was husky. "You kilt my two boys, you sonofabitch," he said.

"And I'm about to kill their father if he doesn't get his hands in the air."

The old man slowly lifted his arms. "You ain't done with me yet, Longarm. I'll still find a way to fix your wagon."

Longarm said, 'Not today and not anytime soon, I don't reckon."

J.J. Hunsacker jerked his head backwards. "There's still some of us out there."

"There is one of you out there—Joe, the last son."

"Then you know that you've still got trouble."

Longarm shook his head slowly. "No, J.J. *You've* got trouble. Joe ain't going to be no trouble to me, not as long as I've got you."

"What do you mean, you murdering bastard?"

Longarm said, "If there's any murdering bastard around here, it's you and we both know that. Now, you're going to tell Joe to come on up here and give himself up."

"What if I just tell you to go to Hell? Would you shoot me down like you did my boys?"

Longarm said, "They were both given the chance to surrender, J.J. You know that. They both got off the first shots, and you know that." The heat was beginning to beat on his back, and he could still feel the weakness in his body. "I'm not going to tell you many more times. I want you to turn around and talk."

Longarm glanced over at Marianne as he gave the old man the order. She was wide-eyed and worried-looking. She had placed herself in between the horses. He would have guessed that Old Man Hunsacker would have liked nothing better than to get a bullet at her. As Longarm caught her eye, she gave him a slow smile, the slightest quiver in her lips. She was brave enough, and more, but it took a strong man, much less a woman, to stand by unarmed while guns were roaring all around you.

Longarm looked at the two men lying on the floor. Now, they didn't seem so dangerous or so bad. One look back at the old man's face as he sat there, deliberating Longarm's instructions, was enough to remove any sense of pity in Longarm's mind. He said, "Are you going to go to the door and do what I asked, or not?"

Hunsacker said, "Go to Hell."

Longarm knew that he had to finish the play in a hurry. Even leaning in the window casing, he could feel his strength ebbing. He needed a long rest. He needed this mess cleaned up. He said, as he lowered the angle of his aim, "Well, Mr. Hunsacker, I reckon if you refuse to do what I tell you, I'm going to have to shoot you in the thigh. If I do that, I'm going to have to break the bone. Now, you wished for me a long, slow death, and I can assure you that you'll have one."

"Oh, yeah? And what are you going to do after you do that? You'll have Joe to deal with, that's what."

"I'm not too worried about dealing with Joe. Are you going to call him up here, or am I going to kill him? One way or the other—it makes no difference to me."

Before he moved, the old man glanced over at Marianne.

He said, "How much money did he promise you, you cheap little whore?"

Longarm said sharply, "Shut up, Hunsacker."

But Marianne said, "You don't have to answer for me, Deputy Long." She turned to J.J. "I didn't do this for money, Mr. Hunsacker, but I doubt if you can understand that. There's a whore in here, all right, but it's not me."

Longarm let the hammer down on his revolver and then pulled it back again—the one sound that people about to be shot find so frightening. He said, thrusting out his arm and aiming at J.J. Hunsacker's leg, only some ten feet away, "Well, what's your answer? Are you going to turn around and go to that door? I'm going to fire in less than ten seconds."

It took Hunsacker only an instant to make up his mind. As if he were spinning on a dime, he suddenly turned, showing his back to Longarm, and said, "There, I'm facing the door. What do you want me to do now?"

Longarm said, "I want you to walk up to that door with your arms down. You're going to call Joe."

Slowly, the old man lowered his arms cautiously, as if he were afraid the movement would draw Longarm's eye. He said, "Like this?"

"Yeah, that would be about right."

"Now what?"

"Now I want you to step into the opening of that door and call Joe down here."

The old man took a few steps toward the door and began to shout. As he did so, Longarm looked toward Marianne and motioned for her to come over. As she worked her way out from behind the horses, Longarm began climbing up through the window. He handed her his revolver as she came near. Their eyes touched as she took the weapon, almost as if she was recognizing the trust he was placing in her. She pointed the revolver at J.J. Hunsacker's back. Longarm clambered over the sill as quietly as he could, but he was weak and it was hard work and he knew it was making his breathing heavier.

J.J. Hunsacker started to look back, and Longarm said, "Keep your eyes outside." He didn't want J.J. to know that there was a woman holding the revolver at him. It might have made him do something foolish.

The old man turned back and yelled, "Joe! Joe! Come on!"

Longarm was inside the cabin. He leaned back against the opening of the window, resting. After a second, he took the revolver from Marianne's hand and nodded. Their eyes met again. Longarm gave her a brief smile. He pushed himself away from the wall, and then walked up behind the old man, taking off his hat as he did so he was not so easily noticed from outside.

He reckoned the last Hunsacker was still a good way out in the desert, but he didn't want to take any chances. He said, "Take a step out that door, J.J. Holler and wave your arms. Tell him I'm done for. Make him come on. Tell him it's all over."

The old man said in a low voice, "I wish to hell that was the straight truth. It still might be—the day ain't out yet. We might still get a chance at you."

"I wish you'd quit wishing me in the grave, J.J. You might be giving me some ideas about you. Now, get it straight in your head, either that boy comes in or you go down. It's your choice. So put some persuasion in your voice with that in mind."

Chapter 11

It was a week later, and Longarm was lying in a bed in a hotel room in Reno. Marianne was lying beside him. He was practically well and almost healed up, even though he still wore bandages on the two wounds in his side. They had been put on by a proper doctor and looked neat, with plaster tape so they wouldn't be slipping all over the place. The doctor had complimented Marianne on the delicacy of her work with the red-hot pocket knife. He'd said, "You got the infection just at the right place, and you cauterized the wound so that it couldn't get reinfected. That was good work. You probably saved this man's life."

But it had still been a time getting from where they had been inside the cabin and into Reno, taking three hard days with two bad prisoners—four if you counted Verlene and Minnie Sewell, both very angry with Longarm for what he had done to their plans and their future. Marianne had tried to talk some sense into them. The Hunsackers had never meant to make any sort of permanent arrangement, but had simply meant to use them and cast them aside when they were no longer valuable or when there was some fast moving that needed to be done.

They had reached Reno, and Longarm had turned the remaining Hunsackers over to the local marshal and the sheriff of the county. In all, he had accounted for eight of the Hunsacker gang. He was delighted to find that his shot at Jim Stock when he was on the elevated platform in the back of the wagon had done the job. Stock had no longer been available to fire his high-powered rifle. The others had fallen as a result of Longarm's bullets as well. Now, the last two were in jail. He and Marianne had survived the mess. He had considered turning Minnie Sewell and Verlene in for any number of infractions, but in the end, he simply cut them adrift and told them both to go their own way.

He glanced over at Marianne. They were both naked, except for the bandages that Longarm was wearing. He said, "You reckon we ought to go down to the dining room and have some lunch?"

She stared up at the ceiling, her eyes lazy and languid. "Right now, I don't think I feel like moving at all. I think I could stay in this bed for another week."

"So could I if I had my way about it, but I don't." In fact, he was leaving the next morning to return to Denver and his boss Billy Vail and his dressmaker lady friend and his regular poker partners. It had been a long time since he had been in his own bed at the boardinghouse where he stayed, and eaten decently for a stretch of time. He was looking forward to it, but he also hated to leave this very interesting woman.

He turned and propped his head up on his hand so that

he could look down and along her body. Her figure was almost as perfect as any he had ever seen. He tried to commit it to memory. Her breasts were like oversized ripe golden apples, topped with dark cherries. The nipples seemed to come out of the rosettes in hard dark cylinders. Then her body fell away to a flat stomach with a tiny navel. There were tiny golden hairs along her body that narrowed down to the mound of golden fleece that rose from the hill where her legs met. Her hips flared out in a provocative way, as did the flat stomach as it gave rise to the perfectly shaped breasts. The hair of the mound was brighter than her other hair, but it seemed to have a tinge around the edges that made Longarm want to put it in his mouth and nibble at it.

They had just finished making love, and he had spent time with her legs wrapped around his head and his face pressed into that moist warm nest. He could still smell the taste of her in his mouth. It was the second time they had made love since they had awakened that morning, both times being a perfect tumble that was wet and warm and full of soaring, aching climaxes that seemed to go on and on and on. He was pretty sure that he had a couple more times in him before they went to sleep that night, but he needed to get some food down and get a little rest.

She looked over at him as if she was reading his thoughts. "You're not tiring yourself out, are you?" she said.

He said, "How can a man get tired of good whiskey, good horses, and good pussy? That doesn't happen."

She smiled and ran her hand through his hair. She said, "Longarm, you are some man. Did you know that?"

"Marianne, I've got a lot to thank you for—a great deal. I reckon you saved my life."

"Well, I can say the same to you. I don't know where I would have finally ended up if you hadn't come along."

"What do you intend to do now?"

She shrugged. "I don't know. Anything but whore. I'm all through with that. In fact, that proposition with the Hunsackers—I had already made up my mind that that would be the last. Of course, I knew we weren't going there to get married. I don't know what Verlene thought, or Minnie Sewell thought, but I knew what it was all about. Now I have no idea but maybe get some sort of job. I've got some money saved."

Longarm said gently, "I could let you have some more. I have a thousand dollars I could let loose if you need it."

She gave him a mocking smile. "I thought you wanted me to quit whoring."

He gave her a stern look. "Hell, woman. Don't twist my words. This would be between friends."

"We are square, Longarm. Get your mind settled on that."

Longarm said, "I don't see it that way, but however you figure it. I wouldn't think you would have much problem snagging a husband if you go to some part of the country where you aren't known. I imagine the young bucks at county fairs would be lining up for you."

She gave him a long, slow look. "Would you be volunteering for the job?"

He answered her seriously. "Marianne, honey, I'm a United States deputy marshal. I can't get married. It just don't go with the job, but if I wasn't what I am, your past wouldn't stop me from marrying you in a minute."

186

She smiled at him and colored slightly. "That may be the sweetest thing anybody's ever said to me."

Longarm looked at her. It had been one of the hardest, roughest, meanest jobs he had ever done since he had been in the Marshals Service, but he had at least had the satisfaction of coming out of it alive having cleaned out the Hunsackers' nest. Perhaps he'd also had a hand in the making of a fine woman. He didn't know when he'd ever been so taken with a woman.

But all in all, he was glad it was over. In a way, he was going to be glad to get on that train the next morning. He said to her as he bent to her lips, "Whatever you do, though, take it slow and be careful."

She curled her arm and pulled his face down to hers. Just before their lips touched, she said, "You're the one who's got to be careful."

In another moment, he understood what she meant.